# The Flood Fighters

by Stephen Dirck

## Albert Payson Terhune

With the original illustrations by Frank Stick

Afterword by Kathryn D. George

Silver
Creek
Press

2015

*The Flood Fighters*
ISBN-10: 0996719415
ISBN-13: 978-0-9967194-1-4

Book compilation and design by Rodney Schroeter.

The Silver Creek Press
PO Box 334
Random Lake WI 53075-0334
rschroeter@silentreels.com

# The Flood Fighters

# Chapter I

THE two boys were fighting. They were fighting for all they were worth. It was a good fight. They were well matched—the greater science of one balanced by the more rugged strength of the other. Yes, it was a good fight and a fierce fight. It was like most of the fiercest fights that are fought in this world. It all started over a silly thing that was not worth fighting about.

The boys were Donald Page and Abel Herrick. They were just fourteen years old, being barely a month apart in age. But in everything except years they were as different as coal is different from hickory. Both of them came from the same section of the Mississippi Valley, too, yet at this first meeting of theirs they were nearly a hundred miles from home.

Donald Page was the only son of the president of the only bank in the river city of Annsburg. Abel Herrick's father was a thriving farmer who lived some six miles out of Annsburg and seldom came to town.

Thus, Don had been brought up a city boy, with every advantage of school and social life that his adoring parents could give him. As son of the richest man in Annsburg, he had been spoiled and petted so long that only his natural spirit had kept him from growing up a sissy.

Abel had had just the opposite kind of upbringing. He had been trained from babyhood to self-reliance and steady work. He had grown up stocky and hard—a complete contrast to the slimly elegant Don.

They met at the big state fair, at Wyckoff, far up the river from Annsburg. As a birthday present and by dint of much wheedling of his nervous mother, Don had been allowed to come up to Wyckoff for the three days of the fair, to visit his father's cousin who had a big country place just north of the fair city. Except for his trips to and from boarding school, this was the lad's first absence from home, unescorted by some member of his family. He was reveling in the sense of freedom from irksome restraint.

Don had a special reason for wanting to come to this particular fair. For one of the exhibits was to be an enormous table which had been brought across country with much difficulty, all the way from California, at his father's expense. It had been bought for a directors' table, to be used in the huge new room that had just been built on the south wing of the Annsburg National Bank. So remarkable was the table that Mr.

Page's cousin—one of the fair's directors and Don's host just now—had prevailed on the bank president to let the mighty piece of furniture break its journey at Wyckoff; there to serve as one of the exhibits.

The big table consisted mainly of two slabs of Sequoía semper-vírens—California redwood—and a stem of the same wood. The slabs were cut each from a single section of redwood tree. The top one, which formed the polished surface of the table, was a fraction over twenty-two feet across. The lower slab, which formed the base, was eighteen feet in diameter and eighteen inches thick—six inches thicker than the top slab. The redwood stem which served as the center leg of the table was ten feet through and the rough reddish bark had been left on it.

The whole table was a curiosity and its presence in the Annsburg bank would be a fine advertisement, since hundreds of people were certain to come flocking to stare at it. So President Page had not really thrown away the fat sum of money he had paid for this central ornament for his new directors' room.

At the fair, for two days, it had been the star exhibit in the Imports Building. Then, on the morning of the third day, one of the hastily constructed roof supports of this building collapsed. In much haste all the exhibits were moved out, lest the entire roof fall in. Room was found for these exhibits in one building or another. Until a proper space could be arranged for the giant table, it was left standing in the open, in the lot between the Imports Building and the river bank, with a special constable to guard it from harm.

And here Abel Herrick got his first look at it. He was destined to see it often enough during the days that were to come; every detail of that table was to be burned into his memory forever. But at first sight it merely struck the boy as a funny monstrosity—much as had the two-headed cow or the 500-pound woman at the side show he had just visited.

Abel had never before been to a state fair. But the brilliant-colored posters that had decked the whole countryside for weeks beforehand had stirred his imagination. He had counted his chicken-and-egg money and had added to it part of the price he had earned from the sale of a shote he had raised himself. With this sum in hand he had gained his father's permission to take a four-day vacation from his chores and to avail himself of a cut-rate excursion to the fair. It was by far the longest trip from home the farm-bred lad had ever taken, and he was taking it alone. Every minute of the jaunt seemed to him a thrilling adventure.

So it was, on his second day at Wyckoff, he rounded the corner of a half-demolished building and came in sight of the great redwood table. Abel stopped short in his tracks and stared. Then, with a grin, he moved nearer.

The hour was five in the afternoon. This corner of the grounds was all but deserted. Moreover, a sudden little rain squall had sent to cover most of the people who were not at the race track or touring the various booths. Just now Abel saw no one near the table but a stylishly dressed boy, slender and a little taller than himself, who was standing close beside it with a very important air of proprietorship.

The boy looked up as Abel came closer. He looked from Abel to the table, then expectantly back again, in the evident hope of hearing or seeing some sign of amazed admiration. But Abel Herrick gave no such sign. In the first place, he did not want the other to brand him as a yap for gaping at a thing which—for all Abel knew—might be as common at fairs as were potato bugs in the Herricks' own truck garden. In the second place, the table did not seem to him anything to admire. It appealed to him only as funny. And his grin deepened as slowly he circled the great double slab and peeped down at the bark-covered stem.

"Well," snapped Donald, irritated at the ever-widening grin. "What do you think of it?"

For reply, Abel merely paused for an instant in his leisurely tour of the table and looked up at the questioner. Then, without answering, he continued to walk about the wide redwood circle. His father had warned him against slick and talkative strangers who might try to engage him in conversation at the fair. Such a person was this other boy. Wherefore, Abel did not speak. But the grin crept back to his freckled face as he noted further the bulging contours of the table.

"That came from California," bragged Donald, resolving to impress this square-visaged and stolid fellow. "It's worth a fortune. There isn't another one like it on earth. It's so valuable that the fair people hired a special guard to watch it. I'm watching it for him till he gets back. He's gone to look for a tarpaulin large enough to cover it, in case this spit of rain should turn into a downpour such as they're having north of here."

Abel paused again in his inspection. This mention of the rain to northward was a subject that interested him at last. Like every other dweller near the Mississippi's banks, he knew what a river flood meant. Again and again from the knoll above his father's barn he had looked out over miles of meadow country that was no longer a meadow, but a swirling part of the overflowed river.

For the past two days there had been all sorts of talk, up here, about the possibilities of such a flood. Farther north, so the newspapers said, torrents of rain had been falling—by far the heaviest rainfall of the year, the dreaded equinoctial storm. The main reservoir at Chatham was overfull and there were doubts as to the safety of its antique dam under the multiple strain. Should the Chatham give way, the volume of waters would rush down into the two lower and smaller reservoirs, probably smashing their dams like so much loose mud, and sending a cataract of billions of gallons of water down into the already dangerously swollen Mississippi. Besides, the river's many upcountry tributaries were even now far above their banks and were adding hourly to the main stream's burden of water. For fifty miles north, along the river, rain was lashing down and increasing hourly the record of flow from every brook and creek.

Abel had heard much talk of all this to-day, and had seen more than one canny fair-goer gather up his family and start homeward toward the safety of the back country. Personally, Abel was not scared at these calamity rumors which the fair authorities were trying to discourage. He did not own any land or any exhibits hereabouts. To him, a flood would mean only an added tang of adventure. But he was mightily interested, just the same.

"Yes," bragged Donald, mistaking his hearer's new air of interest, "this table's worth a fortune. It's the grandest exhibit at this fair. Or any other fair."

"'Tisn't half so funny as the clown, back yonder at the pony-show tent," denied Abel, stung to reply by Don's insufferable manner of superiority, and eager to take him down a peg. "I've seen a pile of funnier sights'n this to-day. A pile of 'em."

"Funny?" gasped the horrified Donald. "Funny? Why, you poor backwoods hillbilly, this table isn't funny! It's—it's impressive! That's what it is—impressive!" he repeated, calling to memory an adjective used by his father in describing the monstrosity. "It's—"

"I pity the poor fool that buys it," commented Abel, jarred by the hated term of hillbilly and beginning to detest this cocksure dude. "'Twouldn't even make decent kindlin', 'pears to me. What's it made of? Stained pine?"

To find out whether or not his guess might be correct, he drew a pin from his coat lapel and scratched an edge of the superpolished surface. Aghast at such a sacrilege, Don leaped forward and with all his force shoved the young vandal away.

"Quit that!" yelled Don. "Don't you know you could be sent to jail for damaging that—that art treasure?"

"I s'pose this fool table b'longs to you?" snorted Abel, recovering his imperiled balance with an effort.

"It's just the same as mine," Don declared. "It will be, some day. It belongs to my father. My father is—"

"You're a liar!" flamed Abel, his hard-held temper going suddenly to smash.

This was the crowning insult—this city chap's assumption that Abel was such a hillbilly as to believe so impossible a yarn.

Putting both hands on the table edge, the country boy vaulted. The leap landed him on top of the table.

"If this yer's your daddy's dinner table," he shrilled, in fierce challenge, "come up here and knock me off'n it!"

Scarce noting what he did, Don made one bound in air—a bound that landed him on top of the table and within reach of the clumsily dancing Abel. He rushed at his foe, head down. Abel ceased dancing and lunged forward to meet the charge. In all his fiery wrath, Donald Page had the wit to remember his boxing lessons. Midway in his rush he halted and shot out his left arm. Abel, both arms spread to grapple with the oncomer, caught Don's left fist square in the mouth and his own head jerked backward as if it were on springs. While he was still dazed, a second blow smote him—this time a cross-body right-hander—in the pit of his stomach. Abel doubled up like a closing jackknife.

Choking back his pain and dizziness, Abel dashed wildly to the assault. Straight through Don's clever guard he tore his way, taking a right hander over the heart without flinching. Then he caught young Page up from the ground in his arms.

Down to the surface of the table he flung his squirming burden. The fall might well have done far more injury than it did had not Abel's foot slipped on the polished expanse of redwood as he heaved. As a result, both boys went to the table top together in a writhing, pummeling, struggling, panting embrace.

They had no eyes or ears or thoughts for anything but each other. In the red battle mists neither of them observed that the shower had all at once changed to a sluicing cloudburst or that the sky was black as dusk. They did not hear cries and running feet from every corner of the fairgrounds as a megaphoned announcement told the pleasure seekers that a long-distance telephone call had just announced the breaking of the Chatham dam. In their obscure corner they battled on, unseen, unthought-of, in the mad scramble of the crowd to get to high ground in advance of the onrushing tidal wave from the north.

Not until the boys swayed perilously in their unloving embrace did Abel chance to look over Don's shoulder to northward. What he saw drove the fury from his brain. Loosing his hold, he gurgled:

"Look!"

Don noted the aspect of horror on the bleeding and puffy face of his foe. He turned to follow the direction of Abel's swollen eyes. Then he, too, forgot the fight, forgot his opponent, forgot everything except that a black mountain was sweeping down upon them from under a blackened sky.

Then before either could cry out or speak or move there was a roar that deafened them. A jarring shock flung them, face downward and still clinging together, to the table top.

In the same instant the table itself was caught up by some incredible power and was spun round and round like a huge top. It rocked like a raft in a heavy sea.

And that was precisely what the enormous table had become—an awkward raft in a heavy sea. The wave had caught it up as though it were a chip and was sweeping it along on the crest of the troubled waters, straight across the low-lying fairgrounds now ten feet under the eddying surge, out into the turbulently pitching yellow surface of the Mississippi.

"Chatham dam's bust!" shrieked Abel into Page's ear, above the churning din of waters. "Just like they said it was due to. This yer table's all that's betwixt us two and a mighty bad way of dyin'. Can you swim?"

"N-no," stammered Don, trying to keep his teeth from chattering and to imitate the other's semblance of calm. "I never learned. Mother was afraid for me to."

"Well," Abel consoled him, "'twouldn't make any great shakes of diff'rence if you could. No swimmer could keep alive a minute in that. Not for one minute. So we'd best stick to this side-show table of your'n till she gives a big enough tip to sling us overboard."

But Don was not listening. His glance had been caught by the appearance of something—at something that seized and held his horrified attention. Pointing a trembling finger at it, he croaked in horror:

"What—what's—that?"

# Chapter II

ABEL followed the general direction of the wabbly finger, shivering in spite of himself at the sudden fright in Don's voice and gesture.

The first glimpse of the object at which the other was pointing did little to calm Abel's own jarred nerves. For a few seconds he stared in open-mouthed amazement.

Through the swirl of yellow waters something was gazing up at them out of the flood. Close to the table edge this shapeless something had upreared itself amid the eddies and waves that beat against the table raft.

From out that shapeless thing shone two dark and agonized eyes. These eyes were fixed upon the boys in an anguish of supplication.

In the gathering darkness the eyes seemed to glow from an inner fire and their expression was human. Yet both boys knew these were not human eyes that were upraised to them in such stark appeal.

The thing was struggling—and struggling for bare life—in the fury of the flood. It seemed to be trying to get to the raft and to the protection of the raft's two scared occupants. As they gaped at the formless thing, it concentrated all its strength into a final struggle that lifted it, momentarily, a foot or so farther out of the water. At the same time it shook itself.

And the shake solved the mystery of the creature's identity by dislodging from its head a tangled mass of weed and muck, through which, until now, only the supplicating dark eyes had shone. As the accumulated rubbish fell away, the head and shoulders of a dog were revealed.

The luckless creature had evidently been caught up by the same monster wave that had swept the boys out into the river. The whirlpools had sucked the beast under and plunged him through mire and flotsam until his head and forequarters were unrecognizable, because of the floating refuse that clung to them.

Now, fighting clear of these impediments, the dog was making a final frantic effort to reach the raft. A right gallant life fight he was waging, there in the waves that washed over his laboring head and the eddies that sucked murderously at his struggling body.

Again and again he was drawn under and always he came to the surface again, albeit more feebly each time, fighting to keep abreast of the fast-moving table, struggling to board it.

A last desperate straining of every worn-out muscle brought him alongside. But he no longer had the strength needed to climb aboard. Indeed, had he been fresh instead of exhausted, he could not well have mounted the ten inches or more of smooth wall that rose above the water and which represented a goodly portion of the top slab's thickness.

Yet he made the effort, like the pure-bred he was, clawing valiantly at the slippery side of the table top and putting every atom of his dying strength into the upward heave. But it was useless. And he sank back, the water closing over his head and shutting from view that awful gaze of anguished entreaty.

Then it was that both boys acted in unison and by one unspoken impulse. As the dog's head vanished under the circling waves, close to the side of their raft, they ceased to be mere gaping spectators of the hopeless struggle.

They flung themselves on their knees, side by side on the tossing and slimy edge of the giant table, and leaned far out, shoving their arms deep under the tumbling yellow surface in the direction whence the appealing dark eyes had just vanished, groping for the drowning dog.

Both of them chanced to find his sinking body at the same time. This, after all, was not so very odd, for the dog had not given up the futile fight, but was still battling against the current that had sucked him under. Hence, he was sinking very slowly, contesting every inch of the way.

Don's groping fingers closed round a handful of thick fur, somewhere in the region of the dog's throat. Abel's stubbily strong grip had fastened on the furry tail. Together the boys heaved, bracing themselves as best they could on the slippery table surface.

For a second there seemed to be much doubt as to whether they were going to haul the drowning dog aboard or whether his weight would drag them from their swaying kneehold into the water. Then a lucky lurch of the redwood slab, as it struck a new whirlpool, lifted that edge of the raft higher out of the river. This added impetus turned the scales in the rescuers' favor, for it hoisted the boys a foot or two skyward, and with them was lifted the body they had grabbed. Backward they floundered, with the sharp counter-pitch of the raft, as it shook free of the whirlpool. Both boys rolled on their backs, atop the table, the drenched and gasping dog above them.

For a full minute they lay there, half stunned by the impact of their jarring tumble, then they scrambled up to their hands and knees and turned their water-blurred stares toward the dog they had rescued. The dog had not recovered so rapidly as had they. He lay sprawling on the raft at full length, the water cascading from off his furry coat, his mouth open in a frantic effort to draw air into his tortured lungs, his sides heaving like bellows, his eyes half shut and glazed. He had fought against fearful odds with every particle of his pure-bred nerve and courage. The fight had left him more dead than alive.

The two rescuers, ignorant of any further way to help him, continued to gaze down in brief silence at the animal they had saved from drowning. He was a collie, tawny and white, mighty of shoulder, daintily aristocratic of head and face and forepaws, his coat as heavy as a grizzly's.

From his neck hung limp a little white linen tag, bearing the half-washed-out number 89.

"Well!" exulted Don, when he could get his breath. "I saved your life, Mister Dog! If it hadn't been for me, you'd have been a goner!"

Abel glowered at the boaster. His own arms still ached from the wrench of yanking the dog aboard. Then, on impulse, he choked back the hot retort that sprang to his lips, as he said:

"You was tellin' me you can't swim a stroke. Was that true?"

"Yes," admitted Don, flushing with a twinge of shame, "my mother didn't want me to learn. She's afraid of the water. I had lots of trouble getting her to let me go boating. Father said I'd best do as she wanted about not swimming, so she wouldn't worry. Her heart's weak. Why did you rub it in by asking?" he finished sulkily, wondering if the other lad were trying to take him down through jealousy, because Don had saved the dog.

"I wasn't rubbin' it in," replied Abel slowly, "I was just sort of thinkin'. You couldn't swim a lick. Yet you took a big risk of goin' overboard, so's to haul that purp aboard. H'm!"

He eyed his fellow refugee with a new and thoughtful interest, the hostility now gone from his freckled face. Donald returned the look. His own thin cheek began to redden.

"Come to think of it," he mumbled reluctantly, "come to think of it, I only pulled half the dog out of the river. You were pulling the other half. I didn't think of that, just at first."

"I reckon you pulled up your share," vouchsafed Abel graciously. "Maybe a wee peckle more."

To shift the uncomfortable subject, he ranged the darkening river with his fight-battered eyes. Then he grunted.

"Away back yonder," said he, " I figgered that whoppin' big whirlpool was due to upset us. Well, we've passed it. See, back there? We went clean through it and passed it. Most likely, when we was wrastlin' with the purp here. If we rode through that whopper, it's like enough the old tub will keep us afloat a spell longer."

"Why wouldn't it?" demanded Don, touched in his pride again, at this slighting mention of the huge table. "It must weigh something like a ton. And the bottom slab is much thicker than the top one. That means it will balance us and act as a kind of keel. If we can stick on, in all these spins and lurches we get, the table will float upright through a tornado. All we've got to do is to stay aboard till the flood goes down or till we're washed inshore and grounded there."

"Inshore?" mocked Abel. "I don't b'lieve there's a square foot of solid shore betwixt here and Noo Yawk City, N. Y.  Look out there, any way you like. You can't see a single thing but water. Except maybe the things that's floatin' on the water. We might's well be in mid-ocean. I tell you we've got to stick to this table-shaped lumber yard, if we can, for a hull passel of days more. I know these river floods. I never saw another one of 'em like this. It's a regular old he-one. We'll be lucky if we aren't in the Gulf, 'fore it lets us ashore."

Don flinched a bit at the grim forecast. Then, rallying, he strove to hide his sudden sinking of spirits by forced ease of manner.

"Well," he began, in a tone he tried to make light, "since we're to be shipmates, or is it tablemates?—from here to the Gulf of Mexico, we may as well start in by getting acquainted. My name's Page. Donald Shelp Page. My father's president of the Annsburg National Bank. I—"

"You don't say!" retorted the other, annoyed once more by the unconscious air of superiority in his new comrade's voice. "Well, Mr. Donald Shelp Page, Esquire, my name's Abel Herrick. That's my name. And my father's president of sixty acres of the cleanest land in Hampden County. Now I guess we're interdooced to each other as good as if Parson Labaw had interdooced us. Shake!"

"Glad to know you, Abel," said Don, trying not to laugh at the country boy's odd speech, which he took for an attempt at culture and whose sarcasm wholly escaped him. "I'm sorry I had to thrash you," he added.

"But—"

"Thrash me?" snorted Abel in swift indignation. "Son, neither you nor all your fam'ly, from Pres'dent Page down, could thrash a quarter section of me! I was just a-warmin' up, when that pesky wave swatted us. It—"

A welcome diversion was supplied at this crisis by a figure which moved between the two youths.

The dog, having regained his breath and a fraction of his strength, had risen laboriously to his feet, stood thus, tottering, for an instant, then came toward the boys to whom he knew he owed his life. It was a timely intervention and it averted the impending clash.

"Good old Towser!" exclaimed Abel, stroking the wet head that was laid lovingly against his knee. "I reckon I'll name you Peter, after a dandy dog dad used to own. Why, that dog—"

"No," contradicted Don, "I think I'll call him Simon. Up at boarding school, one of the fellows had an Airedale named Simon. He was a corker. I wanted father to buy me an Airedale. But mother said she'd read a superstition that they bring bad luck to folks. So I—"

"Simon's a fool name for a dog," criticized Abel with much frankness.

"His name's going to be Simon!" interrupted Don sharply.

Abel shut his lips on a denial. A grin overspread his freckled face. And he said, with meek assent:

"All right. You can have the naming of the dog. And I'll have the naming of this raft. That's fair, I reckon. I'm goin' to name her The Garbage Cart. I—"

"You are not!" yelled the scandalized Donald. "This splendid table cost my father—"

"She's stopped being a table," gently corrected Abel. "She's a raft now. She's the good ship Garbage Cart. And—"

"Oh, go on, then, and call the dog Peter, if you want to!" grunted Donald, sacrificing his will in the effort to save his idolized table from so degrading a title. "Only, don't call this table rotten names. It's saved us from getting drowned."

"All right," acquiesced Abel gravely, while his mouth corners twitched. "We'll kind of compr'mise. We'll call him Simon Peter. There's a man in the Bible named that, you know. And we won't name the raft at all. How does that strike you, Mister Donald Shelp Page, Esquire?"

"Oh, you don't have to call me Mister," said Donald very graciously indeed. "Just call me Don. I shan't mind. I'm—"

"Say!" broke in Abel roughly. "Here we've been standin' round and gassin', like we was on dry land. We're a couple of born fools, spattin' and jawin' like this. We need food and we need fire and we need shelter and it's comin' on dark. Food's first. And it's easiest. The stuff on about a million of the fair tables must be floatin' down this stream with us. We'll lean over, one on each side, and grab for anything that floats along our way and looks eatable. We'll look out for floatin' wood and splinters, too; things that'll make a fire."

Donald, for once in his fourteen years, obeyed a command unquestioningly. The sporting element in this novel form of fishing appealed to him. It was Don who made the first haul—a prize pumpkin.

Next, Abel salvaged a tiptilted crate. Apparently, this hailed from one of the fair eating booths. It held no less than fifteen eggs—the remains of the crate's original five dozen. So carefully were they embedded in their jute packing that scarce one of them was cracked.

With a squeal of exultation Abel salvaged this prize. Scarcely less inviting to his appraising eye than the eggs themselves was the still dry jute wherein they had been packed.

"That means fire!" he crowed. "That and as much of the crate as ain't soaked. And I can get a lot more wood and sich to dry in front of the blaze, when once I get it started. How—how about matches?" he interrupted himself. "Have you got any, Don?"

For answer, Donald fished out of an inside pocket an ornate little silver match box with a hermetically tight top.

"Just one," he reported. "I thought I had more, but—"

"Good!" said Abel, unceremoniously taking the box from him. "I reckon I got a steadier hand than you. When the time comes, I'll light it. We can't afford to lose our only match."

"Where are you planning to build the fire?" queried Don, not relishing the appropriating of his match box.

"Why, where do you s'pose? On the water? We're going to build it right on the center of this yer table and—"

"We are not!" cried Don. "D'you suppose I'll stand by and let you scorch a big black spot in the middle of my father's redwood directors' table? I'm responsible for—"

"Donny," declared Abel with conviction, "if I don't call you a plumb fool it's only because I don't want to insult some real plumb fool by comparin' you to him. Here you stand chatterin' with cold and wet, yet sayin' you won't let me build a fire on it! Well, you got nothin' to say about it. See? I'm goin' to—"

"You're going to give me back that match box of mine!" shouted Don. He advanced on Abel as he talked. In the midst of his words he made a quick snatch for the match box. Abel saw the move just in time to jerk back his own hand which still held the box. Don's fingers missed their mark, but they smote against Abel's knuckles with force enough to knock the silver box to the floor of the raft. Both boys made a rush for it. They collided with a force that sent Abel sprawling.

Don, thrown off his balance, slipped on the polished surface, threw one foot behind him to steady himself —and stepped off backward into the river!

Like a block of lead he plunged straight under the swirl of waters. The raft spun on through the dark. Abel, aghast, struggled up from the floor, babbling incoherently:

"He can't swim a stroke!"

# Chapter III

AS THE unconsciously sputtered words trembled on Abel's lips, there was a sharply hissing and crackling sound, as the table raft plowed its way into the topmost branches of a submerged dead tree and lodged amid the mesh of twigs, swaying groggily to and fro to the tugging of the current.

But Abel Herrick did not heed nor hear the noise of the crackling branches. He scarcely realized the raft had come to a brief halt in its downstream journey. In his whirling brain there was room for but one horrified thought:

Donald had fallen overboard and Donald could not swim.

Acting solely on lightning impulse, not stopping to remind himself that even the stoutest swimmer could scarce hope to live for three minutes in such a mad swirl of waters, he drew in his breath and dived.

Off the table edge he leaped, on the same side that Don had fallen from. His presence of mind was just strong enough to tell him that the flood would have swept Page downstream. Downstream Abel dived. In a second he had come to the surface, in the pitch blackness of the newfallen night, striking out downstream. The rush of the current bore him along with no effort of his own. At his very first stroke, Abel squandered enough of his energy to shout Don's name at the top of his lungs in the faint hope that his companion might still be afloat, buoyed up by his clothes.

A few seconds later he shouted again and this time he heard Donald's voice in an answering hail. Through the roar of water he heard it, not despairingly and as from the throat of a drowning boy, but clear and loud, as though from somewhere above him.

This did not reassure the swimmer in any way. It seemed impossible that Don should be above him and behind him, as the voice indicated. Don must be somewhere in the black river in front of him, his throat already full of strangling water. Then whence came this voice from above and behind? A thrill of superstitious dread swept through the soaked and chilly country boy.

Then came Don's hail again. And this time there could be no doubt as to its direction. Treading water, Abel reared himself shoulder high above the flood and called again. And once more came the answering cry, from some distance behind him and at some point above the surface of the stream.

Abel made shift to turn and start upstream in the direction of the phantom voice. He did not believe Don could still be alive. He did not believe the evidence of his own ears. Yet, if the voice were behind him, there was no use in continuing to swim away from it and the raft. With that same superstitious dread in his heart, Abel set himself to fighting his way upstream.

But struggle as he might, with all his rugged young strength, he could make almost no headway. He felt he was growing weaker and he swam the more vehemently, lying on his side in the turbulent water and using the Australian stroke in order to give as little of his body's resistance as possible to the current.

Now his usually steady nerves began to play tricks on him. The water seemed full of strange creatures that sought to drag him under. Into his dazing mind came the memory of a maxim he had read in a school book and had never forgotten:

"Heroism means holding on one minute longer!"

He held on, swimming with all his waning strength.

All at once a thrill of horror drove the fatigue from him. It seemed he had been right about those river monsters, for one of them lurched forward out of the surrounding darkness and seized him by the shoulder.

In a fury of panic Abel struck at the thing that had gripped his shoulder. His blow missed it in the dark, but his hand, as it drew back again, brushed against a mass of wet fur. At the same time he realized that the creature was trying to aid him in his upstream battle.

"Simon Peter!" he gurgled in a shock of relief. "Oh, good old Simon Peter!"

And now not only the help but the companionship of the great dog nerved the boy to new effort. With the collie gripping his heaving shoulder and fighting upstream with him, his own strokes took on more power.

Presently, though it seemed like a century, his outflung left hand struck against a smooth surface, a foot or less in height. Before he could be certain it was the table raft he had regained, two hands were hauling him upward. Outlined against the murky night skyline he could see Donald Page's slender body, braced in the effort to lift him from the water. As soon as one of Abel's legs was over the edge of the table, Don let go of him and, leaning far out, caught the collie by the ruff. He and Abel hoisted the worn-out dog aboard, before Abel himself was more than half out of the river. Dog and boy collapsed to the wet surface of the raft and lay panting, side by side.

"I tumbled overboard," Abel heard Don explaining disjointedly. "I was just going under when something grabbed me. It was this blessed old dog here. He must have taken a header after me, the second I went over. He dragged me back to where I could pull up over the side. I got up somehow. Then I was just stooping down to help him aboard when I heard you yell out. I answered you and he tore loose from me and swam off, top speed, after you. He's a wonder, that dog of mine—of ours, I mean!"

He stooped, as he spoke and patted the collie lovingly on the wet mass of his ruff. Simon Peter wagged a feeble tail in response. Then Don bent over Abel and helped him to his feet. After which, before Abel could speak, Don held out something toward him. It was the silver match box that had been the cause of the whole misfortune.

"My hand fell on this," explained Don, "as I was scrambling aboard. Take it. You're probably cleverer at building a fire than I am. But maybe you'll let me help."

"Thanks," grunted Abel, still sick and dizzy, as he made his way through the gloom to where he had left the little pile of impromptu fuel.

As he groped over the jute and the driest bits of thin cratewood, Don followed him. Clearing his throat and speaking with some difficulty, young Page began:

"I'd rather be kicked, any day, than to be a fool. I thought this table was too precious to be injured. I hadn't the sense to know that all the tables in the world aren't worth what we've been up against. I acted like a baby. A cranky baby. And it served me right to fall overboard. Then you jumped in and risked drowning, just to save my worthless carcass. If it hadn't been for Simon Peter you'd have drowned, trying to save my life. I—I wish I had a third leg, to kick myself with!" he ended with something like a gulp. "I—"

"Aw, shucks!" growled Abel. "That's all right. Quit gassin' about it and stand between me and the wind. Here's where I light the match—unless you'd rather do it!" he suggested, his heart warming to the lad who had just abased himself so handsomely.

"No, no!" insisted Don. "I'd probably let it go out. Am I standing right?" By way of answering, Abel scraped the match cautiously against the rough bottom of the silver box. His wet coat was held between it and the wind. The match sputtered into a feeble glow. As the boys held their breath Abel nursed the faint flame until it had fairly caught. Then, still shielding it with his coat, he applied it to the loosest strand of jute.

There was an instant's doubt. Then the jute began to flicker. With the lighted match in one hand, Abel shoved the burning fragment of jute under a handful of the same material that he had raveled loose.

For the past five years one of Abel Herrick's morning chores had been the building and lighting of the kitchen fire at home. A thousand times he had wrought over damp wood and bad drafts to get the flame alight. Now the long practice stood him in good stead.

In less than ten minutes a respectable little fire was twinkling through the darkness in the center of the raft. A goodly pile of salvaged firewood was warming and drying, close beside it, sending out clouds of steam.

The two boys cowered over the blaze rejoicing at the welcome warmth that began to replace the numbness of their wet bodies. Before they knew it, they found themselves chatting as intimately as though they had been lifelong friends.

Abel brought forward the salvaged eggs. Each of the boys had six; the remaining three were broken on the raft floor beside the fire for Simon Peter, who licked them up greedily and then crunched their shells.

Don gagged at his first taste of a raw egg. But after he had learned from Abel the simple art of swallowing an egg in one mouthful, he began to enjoy the novelty of it. While the unaccustomed food left him hungry and with a feeling of fullness rather than of satisfied appetite, yet the rich eggs and the warmth of the fire speedily sent new life through him.

Two wet and bruised apples, lifted from the flood, completed the queer meal. After which Abel replenished the fire and the two comrades lay drowsily in front of it, trying not to mind the rain which still filtered down on them. Simon Peter lay between his two new friends, blinking lazily into the comforting blaze and wagging his tail in sleepy appreciation when one or another of the lads patted or spoke to him.

"Maybe some search boat will see our fire," said Abel presently, "and come and take us off. Or maybe it won't. We'd best not count on it. Tomorrow, if we haven't been took off before then, we'll grab up some timbers and things out of the wreckage stuff we go past and fix up some sort of a lean-to. Why, we could live along like this for pretty near a week, if we had to! Kind of fun, ain't it! This is sure one grand table!"

Don made no reply; the lad had cuddled up close to the warmth of Simon Peter's thick coat and fallen asleep. Abel grinned, and curled up to slumber on the other side of the dog.

As he dozed, a slight lurch of the raft and a renewal of the former swaying motion told him that the rising of the river had lifted them free of the tree-top anchorage in which they had been lodged.

At gray dawn Abel awoke. For a minute he lay staring blankly. Then he remembered and sat up to look about him. The motion awoke Don.

Together the boys stared out over the gray expanse of waters. In every direction the river stretched far beyond the range of their eyes. Only an occasional wisp of tree top, here and there, showed land was beneath. Abel wasted little time in viewing it.

Already the country boy was at work over the dying embers of the fire, fanning them to life and replenishing them from the much-depleted store of driftwood. Over his shoulder he called to Don:

"Go fishing! There's breakfast to get. The river's chock-full of things. And lots of 'em's good to eat. Get busy."

The Wyckoff fair had been replete with edible exhibits. Tons of these had been picked up by the tidal wave and flung into the flood. Also, for miles to northward farmsteads had been denuded of livestock and fruits and vegetables by the freshet. The river was alive with a mixed collection of food as well as fuel.

In the course of a half hour Don had salvaged not less than thirty bobbing apples and pears, a score of big potatoes, a cabbage, a flotilla of carrots and onions and turnips and—crowning triumph—an up-ended coop on whose summit crouched six bedraggled Orpington fowls.

Abel had not only restocked the heap of driftwood but had found several wide planks and one or two light joists of timber as well as a board in which were something like a dozen usable nails.

Presently breakfast was assembled. A fat chicken was killed and dressed and cut up. With onions and potatoes it went into the tin pail. Soon a stew was simmering over the coals. There was dearth of seasoning and, when the stew was pronounced ready to eat, the chicken's flesh was more pink than brown. But it was a meal for the gods, for all that.

All day the table drifted clumsily southward on the slowly slackening current. Abel worked valiantly on an improvised lean-to, made of the salvaged boards and similar treasure-trove. Before dusk, with Don's willing but awkward help, he had built something closely resembling a shed—something, at least, that would serve as protection from ordinary rain.

At intervals in the work they played with Simon Peter. Don had been to the fair's dog show the previous morning. From the bench-number tag he knew their collie must have been one of the exhibits.

Next morning found the river still in monstrous flood and revealed to the youngsters no sign of human life amid the ceaseless fleets of wreck stuff. The sun came out in a weakly discouraged fashion.

But daylight brought mishap. Abel had shifted the fire from the raft's center to the side nearest the lean-to, close to the table's edge. Soon after sunrise their bulky craft's bottom slab smote hard against the top of a submerged pine. The jar heaved up one side of the flat surface abruptly to the height of some three feet above water. Then the tree was passed and the raft moved on, but not before the whole side at the edge farthest from the point of contact with the tree top, had been dipped clean under water. With a hiss and a splutter the burning wood slid into the river and the table-edge hearth was drenched by a wave.

"Of all the dad-blamed rotten luck!" raged Abel. "What'll we—"

He ceased grumbling, to peer in dull surprise at Don. Young Page, after a single glance at the devastation, had begun collecting dry jute and other kindling and a wisp of newspaper from the heap of undamaged fuel. As Abel stared, Don drew forth his watch, took off its crystal and held it obliquely above the paper. The sun's rays concentrated through the glass into one gold-white spot on the paper's frayed corner. The paper began to twist and darken under that steady spot. In a few minutes it was ablaze.

"Well, of all the stunts," exclaimed Abel in loud admiration. "Where'd you ever get onto a trick like that, Donny? It's a wonder."

"At the movies," answered Don, delighted that he had for once proved himself the master spirit of the expedition. "I forget the name of the picture. But a couple of fellows were on a desert island. They wanted to signal a passing ship. So they lighted a fire with one of their watch crystals. It's the principle of the burning-glass, you know."

Just after dusk that night they had their first sound or sight of human companionship, apart from each other's, in more than two days. A dense, blinding fog had fallen over the flooded river, making it difficult to see anything ten feet away. Something bumped against the raft. Abel held out a firebrand to see what the object might be. It was a leaky dinghy with a paddle still caught in the thwarts. The boy fastened the boat's rotting rope to a nail of the lean-to.

"Maybe we can row ashore in that," he announced. "Best wait for daylight, though. In this measly fog—"

Through the murk sounded the splash of oars, then the chug of a fast-driven motor boat. As Don filled his lungs for a hail to the passing humans, two shots sounded, then a third.

There was a hideous cry, like the death yell of a murdered man, a resounding splash, as of a body falling from some height into the black water, then silence.

The rowing had ceased. So had the motor-boat's engine.

# Chapter IV

THE collie, at first sound of the mysterious fracas out in the blinding
fog, had sprung to his feet, growling deep down his throat, his deep-set
dark eyes strained to pierce the enveloping murk. Abel, unconsciously,
caught the dog by the collar and stood beside him, head bent forward, to
listen.

Then, out of the silence, came a confused babel of voices. The motor
boat's engine began to hum again. From the diminishing note of the
chugging, the launch was evidently traveling away.

For the first time since the shooting began, Abel remembered to shout.
Their one chance of rescue was moving rapidly away from them. He
filled his lungs and opened his mouth wide, but the breath was expelled
in a soundless gasp.

Over the raft's edge, in the full glow of the firelight, appeared a human
head.

For an instant the boys gazed round-eyed at the apparition. Simon Peter growled fiercely. With instinctive clutch, Abel tightened his hold on the dog's collar.

Then two hands seized the table edge. The raft swayed a little under the new weight. With a mighty effort a man swung himself aboard, sprawling momentarily on the floor of the giant table, while quarts of water cascaded from his well-cut dark clothes.

As he got to his feet, panting from his exertion, Don noticed that a black satchel hung from a strap round his neck.

The man glanced about him, taking quick note of the raft's occupants. He did not speak, but he seemed to be listening eagerly to the far-off hum of the motor.

Then, with no hesitation at all, he strode past Don toward the fire.

Simon Peter seemed to resent this calm intrusion. The dog wrenched free from Abel's slackening grip and made a dash at the stranger. The collie did not bark. He held his head low and snarled in a deadly menace. Abel ran forward to catch him, before he should bury his white teeth in the pallid man of mystery who had boarded their craft out of the night and the fog.

At the dog's first aggressive move the man whipped out an ugly-looking, long-bladed knife from within the breast of his coat. He swung the weapon back in a way that spoke of much practice. Striding forward to meet the dog's assault, he poised the knife for a lunge.

Then, even as his fingers tightened on the hilt and his upraised arm seemed about to descend murderously upon the throat of the springing collie, the knife flew out of his grasp and clattered to the raft.

Donald Page, behind the stranger, had caught up a billet of firewood and had smitten with all his force upon the elbow of the knife-wielding arm. The blow had caught the man athwart the bunch of nerves that swathe the funny-bone. As a result, the fingers, for an instant, had been paralyzed. In the same moment the intruder flung forward his free arm to guard his throat. Into this barrier sank Simon Peter's teeth, missing the jugular only by the width of the shielding forearm.

The man reeled back under the force of the dog's fierce leap. Before Simon Peter could renew the attack Abel had him again by the collar and was struggling hard to hold back the furious beast.

Don meantime had found and picked up the wicked-looking knife. He made no move to return it to its owner, but held it poised in front of him, crouching like a belligerent cat and glaring at the grim-faced intruder.

The man recovered his lost balance and glanced balefully from the snarling collie to the boy with the knife. Then for the first time he spoke. His voice was husky and repressed, as that of a man who for long periods of time had been forced to go without speech or to do his talking on the sly and in a whisper. Yet his intonation and diction were those of a man of education. He had also a very faint German accent.

"What way is this to welcome a half-drowned visitor?" he demanded half aggrievedly, half in an effort at lightness. "Here I climbed aboard your life raft in hope of help and shelter! One of you set a savage dog on me. The other threatens me with a knife. Have I boarded a pirate craft and are you going to make me walk the plank?"

As he talked he kept shuffling his feet as though to stamp the water out of his shoes. And at each shuffle he drew a little nearer to Don.

"I fell into the river," went on the stranger without waiting for either boy to reply. "I fell out of my boat as I was trying to cross to the east bank—if there is any east or west bank left under this flood. As I sank, I saw the glint of your fire through the fog and I swam for—"

"Stop there, please!" interrupted Don. "Stop edging up toward me! If you don't step back there to the middle I'll have to hurry you with this."

And he nodded down at the knife point he was still holding in warlike posture in front of him. The man paused and ceased to shuffle his feet. Over his chalky face for the briefest fraction of a second flickered a look that was not pleasant. Then at once he recovered his self-control.

"Very well," he assented stiffly, stepping back toward the fire. "But I still fail to see why you young heroes treat me as if I were a wild beast or—or—"

"Or a convict?" asked Abel.

The man wheeled on him, scowling. Abel, unruffled, tightened his hold on Simon Peter's collar and explained:

"Up to our neck of the woods there's a feller named Todd—old Cap'n Baldy Todd. He was to state's prison eight years for burglaring, down to Annsburg. I used to know him when I was a kid. And he used to have a big foghorn voice. I was only five years old, but I always remembered that voice of his'n, because it used to scare me so. Well, he come back home last year from the hoosgow, where he'd been all that time. And his big voice had grown to be all soft and flat and whispery—same as yourn, mister. Dad says it got so by havin' to go quiet so long and by talkin' in a queer whisper to the convicts that was next to him in line. Dad says you can pretty near always tell a long-term convict by how he sounds when he speaks. 'Spesh'lly for a spell right after they've been turned loose. Dad says—"

"Your father is right," put in the man quietly and in evident shame, while Don gazed enviously at his chum for supplying this bit of obscure information. "Your father was right. I was released from prison only two months ago. And now," he went on somewhat dramatically, "if you boys are afraid to give shelter to an ex-convict or if you think I am not fit to stay here overnight with you, I'll take my chance of swimming to some log or floating roof. I do not swim well. And I am sick and fatigued and in much pain. But I will chance it, if you say so."

The artistically applied pathos in his voice went straight to the hearts of his unsophisticated audience. The two boys looked at each other in troubled perplexity. Then youthful curiosity came to the fore and Donald asked interestedly:

"What were you jailed for? Murdering someone or just for—"

"I'm not a murderer," declared the man. "I am a poor unfortunate who was foolish enough to want to hold on to my own property when stronger men wanted to steal it from me. They sent me to prison because I wouldn't give it up to them."

"Shucks!" cried Abel in quick sympathy. "That was rotten of 'em! How'd they do it?"

"I see no reason why I shouldn't tell you," the visitor made answer. "It will explain how I happen to be on board this odd raft of yours too."

"Fire away!" exhorted Don, his love for thrilling stories coming at once to the fore. "We'd be glad to listen."

The man looked wearily round him. For only the remotest instant his gaze rested on the knife and on the dog. He said:

"I am drenched and cold and half starved. Can I sit by your fire and dry myself? And if you have any food, can I have a few mouthfuls of it? I can pay for my supper," he added, drawing one or two sodden bills out of his pocket.

"Nobody wants your cash," Abel assured him generously. "This grub didn't cost us anything. And even if it had we wouldn't take money for feedin' a hungry man."

The man sat down, willingly enough, on a low crate beside the blaze, his hands and feet stretched to its warmth. Don, still gripping the beloved and terrifying knife, stood melodramatic guard over him, while Abel rummaged their improvised larder for cold provisions. Donald called across to his busy friend:

"Here's some real life that's just like the movies, Abel. This gentleman came aboard just as he might have done on the screen. And did you see the way I got the knife away from him? I learned that in a movie serial called The Billion Dollar Bride. The villain drew a knife on the hero. The heroine crept up behind him and hit him that way on the funny-bone with a piece of skeleton. They happened to be in a wild beast's den at the time. If I hadn't gone so much to the movies—"

He checked himself in his joyous bragging and said less smugly:

"But then it was you who knew about the convict voice. It was clever of you, Abel. I—"

"Shucks!" interposed Abel, handing the food to their guest; "that wasn't anything. Go ahead and eat, stranger. Then we want to hear that jail yarn of yourn. It's got me puzzled what it can have to do with your boardin' us to-night."

Possibly it had the visitor puzzled, too, for as he ate it seemed almost as though he might be casting about in his agile mind for a story that would fit the case.

By the time he had finished bolting his meal, he seemed at ease. He glanced across the fire to where the two boys were waiting eagerly for the promised tale.

Don held the knife, though less truculently than before, but the expression of the collie's dark eyes as they rested on the stranger was still hostile. The man cleared his throat.

"In the first place," he began, "my name is Desmond. Claude C. Desmond. I am an inventor. I—"

"I thought Desmond was an Irish name," interposed Donald. "You talk like a German. Is—"

"I went to a German university," explained Desmond. "My parents were Irish-Americans. I picked up a shade of German accent, I suppose, at Heidelberg. But—"

"My uncle Gerald went to Heidelberg," said Don. "He didn't get any

German accent there. He—"

"Aw, shut up about your uncle!" commanded Abel impatiently.

"I am an inventor," went on Desmond smoothly. "Five years ago I"—staring out into the mist as if for inspiration—"I invented a fog-dispersing device."

"A—a which?" asked Abel uncertainly.

"A fog-dispersing device," was the glib reply. "Fog is a mariner's most dangerous foe, both on rivers like this and on sea. Ship owners would gladly pay tremendous sums to have their vessels equipped with it. It would save millions of dollars and thousands of lives. Well, I had toiled and puzzled and studied over the problem since I was a boy. That was why I went to the scientific school at Heidelberg. And at last, five years ago, I hit on the secret.

"I was foolish enough to tell some friends about it before I had patented my invention. The word got out. A syndicate of rich and unscrupulous men heard of it. They saw the immense fortune in it. And they made me an offer for the model of my apparatus. It was a petty offer. I refused. Then they resolved to steal the bag in which I kept the model and the papers.

"But I watched the bag too carefully," continued Desmond. "I dared not send it on to the patent office, for fear they might rob the mail. When the syndicate found the precious bag could not be stolen, they trumped up a forgery charge against me, hoping to steal the invention while I was helpless in prison. But I got word of it just in time to hide the bag away in a safe place. They had me tried, on their perjured evidence, and sent to prison."

"You poor cuss!" grunted Abel.

"All the time I was there," went on Desmond, after a short pause, "they hunted for that bag. When I got out, I knew they would be watching me. I waited for nearly two months before I went near the place where it was hidden. I thought I had thrown them off the track. But I hadn't. This noon, I reached the river. I had just found a boat that had been washed ashore in the flood and I got into it and started to row across. As I set out from shore, I saw five men break cover and run down the bank after me. They were a gang of toughs hired by the syndicate to trail me. In a few minutes, it seems, they found a motor boat somewhere.

"After me they came," said Desmond. "I thought I was a goner. But just then the fog settled down. They lost me. For hours I rowed about. Then, in the dark, I blundered right into them. And they opened fire on me. My only chance was to dive. And I did. I suppose they thought one of their bullets had killed me and that I had fallen overboard and sunk. When I came to the surface I saw the light of your fire, and I swam toward it. That is all. Except," swinging forward the black satchel that swung from his neck, "except that my invention is safe!

"Now," finished Desmond, "if you don't mind, I'll stay here till the fog lifts. My enemies think I am dead. So perhaps I can make my way with this treasure to the Patent Office at Washington, before they learn better. Once let me get this safely patented and—"

"Only," demurred Donald, "why did you draw a knife on us, the second you got here? That wasn't—"

"My eyes were blurred with the water and the fog," said Desmond. "How could I tell you weren't another party of toughs sent out by the syndicate? All I saw was a dog rushing at me and—"

"We're with you!" declared Don with much enthusiasm. "We'll see you through. What'd I tell you, Abe? Didn't I say real life was just the same as the movies?"

"My dad is a mighty wise man," Abel ruminated, speaking for the first time in some thoughtful minutes. "And whenever I used to tell him a lie, when I was little, he knew it was a lie, no matter how slick I told it. When he'd broke me of lyin', he told me how to know if a feller is lyin' to you or not. He said a liar may be able to manage his face while he's springin' his whopper, but he'll always clinch his hands tight. Now, this Desmond person has told us a reel int'restin' yarn. But all the time he kept his hands so tight clenched that his fingers were white to the knuckles. He can stay here along with us till mornin', but," picking up the knife Don had just laid down, "one of us'll keep guard on him with this pigsticker till daylight. How do we know but what it was him that stole this fog machine from some other man and that the other man was a-chasin' him when he dived overboard? Hey, Don?"

Don, after a moment's profound consideration, agreed. Abel was to stand guard until two in the morning.

At two, promptly, Abel waked his sleep-sodden chum and handed him the knife. As Abel rolled over in the lean-to, Don looked at Desmond. The man was lying moveless, his eyes shut, his breathing slow and rhythmic.

For half an hour Don watched. Then his own head began to nod.

"I can guard him just as safely lying down," the boy told himself.

He stretched himself out beside the fire. Five minutes later, the boy was asleep. In another half hour Desmond stirred—furtively and craftily—not at all like a newly awakened slumberer.

## Chapter V

THE fog was still thick and heavy, lying like a wet woolen blanket, when Abel opened his eyes. A weird grayish light over the swollen river proved to him that morning had come. He stretched himself and sat up. Simon Peter, who had crawled into the lean-to and had gone to sleep at his side, also woke and got to his feet.

The first sight that met Abel's blinking gaze was Donald Page, lying dead asleep beside a heap of ashes and charred wood. The fire was out, clean out, thanks to the negligence of Don, who had been supposed to replenish it during his hours of guard duty.

This was the thought that smote athwart the sleep mists in Abel's half-awake brain. The idea of guard duty started another train of thought. Desmond! At once the boy was wide awake.

Abel stared about him, over the flat table top. Desmond was not there! The lad sprang up and ran over to his peacefully slumbering chum.

In the midst of a wild dream of turning a rapid-fire fog-disperser upon a band of syndicate-hired ruffians, Don was brought back to the realities of life by a savage shake that drove the breath from his lungs. He looked up, mumbling and protesting, to find Abel standing over him, white with rage.

"You pesky dude!" stormed Abel. "You lazy, good-fer-nuthin' shote, you! You ain't worth your feed and you never will be! If this was wartimes, the gen'r'l would have you shot for this. And I'd be tickled to death to stand by and see it done. You wall-eyed city mucker, look what you've gone and done! You're a sweet-scented cuss to leave on guard, ain't you?"

During the whirlwind of abuse that burst over his dizzy head, Don Page had scrambled to his feet, his heart wrathful at the rude disturbing of his rest and at the vituperation hurled upon him. He had opened his lips to make vigorous and furious retort, when the words, "to leave on guard" struck a note in his drowsy memory. He, as Abel had done, peered about him in the fog.

"Where's—where's Mr. Desmond?" he sputtered. "I didn't dream it, did I? He—"

"No," mimicked the raging Abel, "you didn't dream-it-did-I! It happened. But you spent the rest of your time a-dreamin'. And he got away. So did the fire. Now, if you can stop dreamin' for a spell, s'pose we go see what else, maybe, is gone!"

Without deigning to waste more time over the recreant Donald, he started on an inspection tour. A second later, he made his first report.

"Dinghy's gone," he called over his shoulder. "Its rope's cut. He didn't even bother to wait to untie it before he got aboard. Cut it with his own knife most likely. The knife you was s'posed to be guardin' him with! Took it right out of your hand while you was asleep. Pity he didn't roll your carcass over into the river, while he was about it! Prob'ly he had too much mercy on the poor harmless fishes."

Abel broke off his denunciation with a howl, as he discovered that the carefully stocked larder was all but cleaned out. The chickens were gone. So were most of the vegetables and fruit. So were one or two other more or less useful bits of flotsam salvaged with much care during the past two days.

Evidently Desmond had stocked his dinghy for a long trip.

Don, meantime, was feeling instinctively for his watch, a gold timepiece which was his chief treasure and joy and which had been a gift to him from his father on his recent fourteenth birthday. Always, on awakening, he consulted this watch. He had been delighted that it had escaped injury during his brief immersion in the river. And he had kept it wound with absolute regularity during the short voyage.

The watch was gone.

So were forty-one dollars in bills that he had carried in a vest wallet. Don groaned aloud. At the dolorous sound, Abel turned.

"Playin' baby won't get you nowheres," adjured Herrick. "You let Desmond get away. And you let the fire go out. And you let him steal our boat and most of our grub. It ain't for you to do the moanin'. That's my job. If—"

"He stole my watch," said Don, trying to steady his voice. "And all the allowance money I'd saved up."

Abel's glower vanished. That watch of Donald's had seemed to the country boy the most magnificent and costly bit of jewelry on earth. The news of its loss drove from Abel's mind all the sting of resentment against his plundered chum. The disappearance of the forty-one dollars—more ready money than Abel had ever possessed at any one time—completed the dispersal of his wrath.

"Gee, but I'm sorry!" he cried, coming up to the despoiled youth. "And here I was grouchin' over us losin' a leaky old sieve of a dinghy and a handful of grub! Hard luck, Donny! I'm plumb sorry I was so cranky. I—"

"You needn't be sorry for the way you yelled at me," said Don, taking fresh grip on his self-control. "I had it coming to me, all right. I was left on guard. And I went to sleep at my post—like the sick soldier I saw in the movies. I deserve to get robbed."

"No, you don't, neither!" denied Abel, a lump in his throat. "And you take it fine too!"

"You're the one that's taking it fine," said Don. "Here we've lost the boat and the fire and all the food you've been storing up! And yet you have time to be sorry for me! Oh, Abe, I'm a mucker! Just as you said. That's what I am. A mucker! Let me tell you something. And then you can kick me if you want to. When we first got on this raft I thought you were just poor white trash. I figured I was seven million times better and brighter and finer than you were. I figured I was doing you a favor to let you associate with me. Honestly, I did, Abe. Then what did you do? First you hopped overboard to try to save me from drowning, even though you knew it'd probably mean your death. Then you kept us alive and comfortable here where I'd have starved and got chills. Then, when I wanted to trust that crook of a Desmond, you kept me from doing it. And you stayed awake and on guard half the night—I couldn't even do my share of the guarding for half an hour! And now, instead of smashing me for all the loss I've caused us, you—you're behaving like—like—Oh, Abe, you make me feel rottenly ashamed!"

"Shut up!" roared Abel, a foolish break in his voice. "Shut up, you! If you've learned a wee peckle from me, ain't I learned a sight more off'n you? Who lit the fire by a burnin' glass when I'd have never knowed how? Hey? Who done that? Who knocked the knife out'n Desmond's hand and kept old Simon Peter from gittin' stabbed and maybe kept us both from gettin' our throats cut? Who's takin' the loss of his dandy watch and his cash like a white man and teachin' me a lesson in not whinin'? If it comes to that. Aw, shucks! Cut out the mushy talk and let's see what's left to us!" he ended, his voice thickening.

He turned away, with all a normal boy's embarrassed dislike for sentiment. Feeling in his own pocket, he produced his large nickel watch and four dollars and fifty-five cents.

"He didn't go through me," commented Abel. "I wonder why. I know!" he interrupted himself. "I know why. Simon Peter had crawled in to sleep beside me—like he always does. The dog saw we wasn't enemies of Desmond's. So he went to sleep and didn't bother to watch him. But Desmond wasn't takin' any chances on Simon Peter's wakin' up and findin' him rummagin' through my clo'es, right alongside him. So, I take it, Desmond moved stealthy-like, not to wake the dog, and he kept to the other side of the raft. Anyhow, we've still got a burnin' glass, if ever there's any more sun. And we've got enough cash to get us both home by train—and Simon Peter, too—if ever we strike land. Now come on and help me fish for some more grub and firewood."

For the next hour they were busy at their favorite river pastime of salvaging foodstuff and fuel. But to-day they were much farther downstream than before. The produce from the fair and from water-side farms had had time to spread out into thinner area or to pass the raft or to be passed by it. Wherefore their luck was lean. Wood of all sizes and sorts was as plentiful as ever. But food was not.

The hour's fishing netted them an abundant store of fuel and two long poles which they stowed carefully on board against the time when the river should be low enough to let them guide or propel the raft by punting, but in food it brought them only four apples, a mammoth squash, some onions and three potatoes.

At last, chilled and famished, they desisted and prepared to make such scanty meal as their assets would permit.

"I read a piece in the Annsburg Clarion," said Abel, breaking a long silence as he began to slice a cold and clammy onion with a view to beginning his breakfast with it, "a piece in the Woman's Page, where it said raw onions was fine for the c'mplexion. So here's where I snare me some fine c'mplexion. Say, Donny, we got rid of Mister Desmond dirt cheap. Honest, we did. If he'd stayed here, he might 'a' knifed us or throwed us overboard or some of the fellers that's after him might 'a' found us and thought we was in cahoots with him and jailed us. Yes, sir, we're dern well rid of that cuss at the price! He—Look-a-yonder!" the boy broke off, dropping his detested and half-chewed onion, to point at something half a mile or more downstream.

The fog had begun to thin as the morning wind whipped across the river and through a vista thus opened the boys saw a low-lying splotch of land that showed black and indistinct in midstream, directly in the path of their wallowing raft.

While they gazed at the faintly outlined mass of darkness on the gray-white surface of the water, the wind freshened with a sudden gust. As by a miracle, the fog scattered before the singing little gale.

"Yon's an island!" proclaimed Abel. "There's lots of 'em, hereabouts, in the old Mississip'. We're headed dead on for it too! The luck's a-turnin', Donny. In another hour, at this rate, we'll be steppin' on solid ground. Likewise," he added, as an inspired afterthought, "that Desmond chap has sure done us one good turn without meanin' to. See how the mist's all scatterin' away? That means he's set his fog-disperser to work, somewheres. It's one mighty slick machine for all it was invented by a skunk. It's workin' grand!"

"Suppose Desmond is on that island?" suggested Don worriedly.

"Well, then," assented Abel with valiant carelessness, "what if he is? He's got that knife. But we got these two long boat poles, haven't we? And we got Simon Peter, haven't we?" stroking proudly the collie's silken head. "We're more'n a match for him. A whole lot more. If he's there, we'll take a pole apiece and light into him and sick Simon Peter onto him at the same time. I'm reckonin' he'll be glad enough to hand back that watch and money of your'n, before we're done with Mister Claude C. Desmond, Esquire. Hey, Simon Peter?"

The collie wagged his plumy tail in grave acquiescence to the question—whatever that question's meaning might chance to be. Already Simon Peter had adopted the two castaways as his gods, his worship having begun when they lifted him from the water as he was sinking from exhaustion. He whom a pure-bred collie once accepts as his god is forever that dog's god, to be served and loved and guarded and fought for, while life lasts.

The sight of the island had thrilled both boys with the magic zest of discoverers. The possibility of encountering Desmond there lent a delicious tang of strife and peril to the coming adventure.

"Claude is a funny first name for a man, outside of a book, to have," remarked Abel presently, too nervous with anticipation to keep quiet.

"Oh," argued Don, pausing in his task of wielding the plank oar, "Claude isn't an uncommon name at all. I've seen it dozens of times in the movies. But," he hurried on as Abel frowned, "the cashier of my father's bank told me once that when a man is making up a false name to use, nine times out of ten he'll take C for a middle initial. I don't know why. And Mr. Desmond told us his name was Claude C. Desmond. So perhaps—"

"'Tisn't an island, at all!" cried Abel, whose eyes, keener than Don's, had been boring into the ever-nearing blot of darkness ahead of them. "And it can't even be in the river. It's 'way up on land somewheres—where the land gen'r'lly is, I mean. See?"

Don bent his own gaze on the line of darkness, screwing up his lids and shading his brow with his hand. Gradually the supposed island began to take definite form to him.

One of the several eccentric currents of the overflowed river had evidently set strongly to eastward, shoving an avalanche of flotsam with it, and sucking in more and more wreckage from the less rapid-moving portions of the stream as it sped on.

This current had swept through a wide but shallow grove of tall pines and other trees, somewhere on the bottomlands close to the river's usual bank. The grove, lying broadside on to the stream, with the top branches of its trees almost touching one another, had served as a monster net. In its evergreen meshes had lodged tons of floating wreckage. As more flotsam arrived, the force of the current had pushed the earlier driftage tightly against the screen of boughs, forcing some of it nine or ten feet under water and against the thicker and more resisting parts of the trees, then piling up new material on this close-packed foundation.

Thus had been formed a practically solid island, more than two hundred yards wide, perhaps fifty yards thick.

To the boys' wondering senses, samples of everything they had ever seen on or round the Mississippi were lodged here.

Barn roofs, boat-yard stuff, smashed sheds, parts of haystacks, scantling from unfinished houses, boxes, crates, barrels, kegs—some full, some mere broken shells—half-acres of bobbing vegetables and fruit, a myriad fair-booth gewgaws—everything imaginable that would stay above water, from an upside-down baby carriage to a newly arrived gilded dragon which had decorated the entrance of the fair's large circus tent.

"It's better'n all the sure-enough islands that ever happened," Abel exulted, plying the plank oar with wild energy. "We c'n tie up there for keeps. It'll keep us fed and sheltered and ev'rything and we c'n have more fun than a goat, explorin' round. Folks'll be sure to see that island sooner'n they'd see a raft. And the first search party will come and take us off. Or some of them four or five upset boats yonder along the edge may be sound. If they are, we c'n row to shore right off. Glory be!" he shrilled. "Look-a-yonder on that tilted-over ridgepole, there to the left. If there ain't more'n fifty chickens an' turkeys a-roostin' there, all wet and huddled up in bunches, I'll—I'll eat 'em raw! Now, then, see if you c'n swing her a little more to the left, Donny. We're headed dead on, but I'd hate to run a chance of missin'. So!"

As he spoke he braced himself against the raft's lean-to and slung the loop of their remaining length of frayed rope over the outjutting top of a dead pine that projected six feet above water in the vanguard of the submerged grove. The raft swung gently to port, shoved by a last push of the tide, coming to a halt against the half-sunken roof of a boathouse. Eagerly the boys worked to secure the table even more staunchly to the island's edge. A minute later their labor was completed.

"Now for the exploring!" cried Don, chattering with the thrill of it all. "Say! I've got an idea! There's a boat, see? Right over there beyond your side of the table. We can reach it easily. Let's find if it is still any good. If it is, we can get inside it and row all round the island. There's lots to be seen on the other side, I bet. And if we have the boat we won't need to climb over all that mountain of stuff. How about it?"

Already Abel was reaching out a pole toward the overturned little boat whose bottom was well above water.

"Perhaps we can find some oars too," said Don as they pulled the upset boat toward them. "If we can't we can paddle with a plank or— Abe!" he shouted as with some effort they righted the craft, "do you know what boat that is! It's the dinghy we found yesterday—the one Desmond stole and got away in!"

"Upside down!" Abel gasped. "Oars gone too. Except that steering paddle. Look! It's still sticking to the bottom where we strapped it."

He reached under the stern seat, to unfasten the loop of twine whereby he had secured the paddle's handle to a protruding nailtop on the keel's stern. Then he withdrew his hand far more quickly than he had thrust it beneath the hood-like seat. In his grasp, as he withdrew his fingers, was a bag.

"Remember that valise!" he exclaimed. "It was jammed there, just now, between the seat bottom and the stern. It stayed safe all right. A heap safer'n he did, poor feller! He's gone. And his fog-dispersin'

machine is all that's left of him. It was—it was kind of like Providence,"
he added sheepishly, "that we happened along here and found it. Maybe
it was intended we should save it for—for mankind, as the sayin' is."

Don eyed the bag keenly.

Gingerly he fumbled with the lock of the valise. After a few experi-
mental tugs, the bag's mouth flew wide open.

Both boys stared tensely into the receptacle. Then on their eager faces
the aspect of curiosity faded to utter blankness. And an expression of
horrified wonder in turn displaced the blankness. Abel was the first to
get his labored breath.

"Suff'rin saints!" he croaked, his throat sanded and contracted.
"He—he said it was—said it was a—a machine!"

# Chapter VI

THE sun broke gayly through the nest of clouds that the wind was scattering. A golden ray of sunlight smote sharp on the wide-opened bag into whose recesses the two lads were staring, bringing into clear view the satchel's tumbled contents.

At first glance the receptacle seemed to be crammed with roll after roll of paper money. There were fully a dozen such rolls, of varying sizes and hues, each strapped by a rubber band.

Probably, the bills had once been stacked in some semblance of order. But the tossing of the dinghy and Abel's rough attempts to open the bag had piled the rolls into a confused mass, one atop another or scattered from end to end of the small satchel. This very carelessness of arrangement multiplied the impression of enormous wealth.

After Abel's first involuntary outcry, neither he nor Don spoke for at least a minute. Heads close together and eyes abulge, they squatted, side by side on the raft-edge, devouring with their dumfounded gaze the high-heaped fortune before them.

The country boy had never in all his fourteen years beheld nor dreamed of so much real money. The sight of it took his breath away and left him weak and dizzy.

Don, at the Annsburg bank and once during a visit to the Philadelphia Mint, had, of course, seen far larger amounts. But they had never struck him speechless as did the spectacle on which his eyes now feasted nor had they filled him with that queer breathless and tingling excitement.

For a space the two gloated, speechless.

It was Abel Herrick who first regained a semblance of sanity. His sturdy nerves and sturdier common sense resumed control over his dazzled mind.

"That feller," he began, speaking slowly and trying to marshal his facts in due order—"that feller said the bag held a model for a machine to disperse fog. He lied. It's chockablock with billion-dollar bills. I'll betcha there's more money in this-yer bag than there is in all the rest of this state. He's at the bottom of the river now, and I hate to call a drowned man a liar. But he was one. How'd we come to meet him? There was a rowboat chased by a motor boat. We heard the oars and we heard the motor. Then we heard them shots and a splash. Then, after a spell—while most likely they was lookin' for the feller that had fell overboard—we heard the motor boat go on. That proves the feller who jumped overboard was the one in the rowboat."

"But—"

"'Cause there wa'n't any more sound of oars. And Desmond come aboard. He was chased, like he said, and he dived, at the shots, like he said. But he wasn't runnin' away from ruff'ns. He was a thief runnin' away from the p'lice and a-totin' his plunder along with him. If he'd 'a' been square he'd never 'a' told us that fog-dispersing whopper. Nor yet he wouldn't 'a' sneaked off with your cash and your watch, Donny. I reckon when he left us he was in such a hurry and the fog was so thick, he rowed this-yer dinghy plumb into one of them big logs that's been strewin' the river ev'rywhere. The dinghy is just a cranky, wabbly scow that'd turn turtle if he batted an eye in it. Over goes the boat. And over goes he. He can't find the upside-down dinghy in the fog and he drowns. Anyhow, he never got to this-yer island. If he had, the first thing he'd 'a' saw would be the dinghy with his bag of money in it. He—"

The boy's voice trailed away. Hard as he had tried to think logically, he could no longer fix his mind on anything but the rolls of wealth in front of him. He fell to staring at it again.

"Of course," said Don presently, lifting his eyes with an effort from the contemplation of the money, "of course, Mr. Desmond may have been an honest man—a bank messenger or a paymaster for some construction company up-river. He may have been on the way to deliver the money when the thieves got after him. Maybe he didn't trust us and that was why he told about the fog-disperser and—But I'm talking like a fool. He stole my watch and my allowance money. Of course he was an escaping thief. You were right, Abe. Besides, we know he was a convict. He—"

"Billions and billions of dollars," babbled Abel dreamily, still surveying the bag with rapture.

"At the Philadelphia Mint," denied the other, "they let me see a package that held a million dollars. It was ever so much larger than that bag. There can't be so much as a million dollars here. Let's—let's count it. Shall we?"

This fascinating proposal took Abel by storm. In the bliss of such occupation the boys forgot hunger and fatigue, forgot the presence of foodstuffs, forgot everything except the enthralling process of counting their hoard of treasure trove. They divided the rolls of bills evenly between them. Then each began to count, opening roll after roll and noting the amount of money in each by penciled figures on the table surface.

Don, from his frequent experiences in watching money counts at the bank, told Abel how to pile the bills in separate sheaves, all of each denomination in a pile by itself. With bits of water-logged wood they weighted these fast-growing sheaves. It was not a hard task.

Then, for many minutes, there was complete silence, save for the riffling of the crisp or limp bills, the inaudibly whispered counting and the occasional scratch of a pencil on the raft-edge.

It was Donald Page who finished first. Not only were his fingers and his brain more alert and practiced than were those of his chum, but the frequency of his former views of money in large quantities led him to pause less often, to stare in bewildered ecstasy at the treasure. So his half of the bill rolls was counted and the totals were added correctly, long before Abel's share of the delightful labor was done.

"Six thousand, four hundred and thirty dollars!" he announced, putting the sheaves of notes together again and binding them with the largest rubber band.

He tried to make his voice sound natural and matter-of-fact as he spoke. But it shook in spite of him.

"Six thousand and seventy dollars!" said Abel, a few minutes later, speaking in a hushed undertone.

"That makes," computed Donald, figuring rapidly, "just twelve thousand five hundred dollars."

He and Abel looked in owlish solemnity at each other, their overburdened brains trying to grasp this stupendous fact. For, while they had talked glibly enough of millions and billions, yet the actual presence of $12,500, as a concrete fact, proved all but appalling.

Finally, Abel spoke. His lips had been moving wordlessly for some seconds.

"Donny," he said in awe, "that means that you and me are worth $6250 apiece, in cold cash! It sounds like it was crazy talk. But it's gospel, for all that. This money's our'n. Your'n and mine, Donny! If 'twas stole, we didn't steal it. If 'twas Mister Desmond's, he's at the bottom of the Mississip'. It b'longs to them that found it. That's us. You and me, Donny. We're—we're rich men, friend!"

"Yes," assented Don, as he drew his breath in with a long and quivering sigh of wonder, "we're rich! And it's ours by rights. The man who had it is dead. If he stole it we can't be expected to go round to all the people he robbed and ask how much he took. We couldn't find them, in the first place. If it was his own honest money—well, we're pretty sure he gave us a wrong name. So we can't very well write to his relatives and his heirs and his lawyer. We wouldn't know whom to write to. The money is ours. You're right. Over six thousand apiece. What can't we buy with that? Just think! I spoiled the little motor boat my father gave me by leaving it badly moored, so it drifted over the rapids down near Mitch Dawes' and was crushed. Father said I must wait till I could save enough money out of my allowance before I could have another. I can get one now; I can get a corking one. And I can get—"

"Dad's honin' for that ten-acre corner of bottom land," mused Abel, "the one Jim Ludlum wants to sell. And he's got a dandy chance to buy Micken's tractor if he can put up the ready cash right off. I reckon my share will pay for both of them things. And when we get goin' with 'em then watch our farm take a jump! Maybe there'll be enough left over for—"

"I can get another watch, too!" cried Don, suddenly discovering a new use for his fortune. "Just like the one Desmond stole. And maybe with a repeater attachment in it, like father's watch. And —"

"Hold on!" exhorted Abel, fondling the money in his lap. "First thing we do is this: We take out of each of our shares half the price of that watch you lost and half of the forty-odd dollars he swiped. Then we'll start fair; Desmond will be payin' his debts that way too."

"No, no!" expostulated Don. "We're not going to take any of it out of your share, Abe. We're—"

"I'd feel better, that way," declared Abel. "Anyhow, we c'n jaw over that later. I'm starvin'. Let's rustle some grub. There's enough of it here to feed us for a month."

Reminded of his own latent hunger, Don joined gladly in the food hunt. The money was returned to the bag and the bag was hidden at the back of the lean-to. The boys invaded the hither edge of their island on a breakfast foray.

Within an hour, a fat hen was bubbling in the pail kettle, along with a lot of vegetables. A wooden biscuit box supplied them with plenty of crackers. Other boxes and barrels and crates had been rifled of something like a hundred pounds of varied provisions which were now stored in the lean-to along with the ten large chickens and a couple of turkeys. A fair-booth cook-kit, dug out from a pile of brushwood, supplied them with several cooking and eating implements and with an abundance of salt and pepper. A floating quarter-barrel of sugar was next salvaged. The cook-kit provided a good-sized box of matches among its other loot.

"Now, then!" chuckled Donald, as at last they sat down to their savory meal and heaped a wooden plate with stew for Simon Peter. "Home was never like this!"

"Eat hearty!" responded Abel, his mouth full.

But, when the first pangs of famine were satisfied, Abel pushed aside his food glumly. His usually ravenous appetite was not up to the mark. Nor had his square face the aspect of jolly contentment that it was wont to wear. Every now and then he glanced uncomfortably toward the lean-to where the satchel was hidden.

Then, in furtive fashion, he looked at Don. His chum's face was as gloomy as his own. And Don's plate was not half emptied. Abel swallowed hard. Then his mouth twisted as if with toothache and he burst forth sourly:

"Aw, shucks! I know what you're a-grouchin' about! And you're dead right. We're a pair of skunks, you and me, and I'm the worst of the two. 'Cause it was me that said it first."

"What—what do you mean?" quavered Donald, with a bad attempt at ignorance.

"You know blame' well what I mean!" growled Abel. "That money ain't our'n. We got no more right to it than the man in the moon. If we was to keep it we'd be as much thieves as that cuss, Desmond. The money ain't our'n."

Don frowned portentously at his friend's foolish change of heart, but under the troubled flicker of Abel's steady eyes broke down.

"You're right!" he confessed, almost with a groan. "And I've been trying to pump up the courage for half an hour to say the same thing. It isn't our money."

Abel glanced across at his chum. Their eyes met. Then, by wordless impulse, their hands met in a hard and embarrassed grip. After which, ashamed of their momentary sentiment, they fell upon their neglected breakfast with appetites that had all at once become as keen as recently they had been blunt.

"I tell you what let's do," suggested Don, breaking silence, as he swallowed the last mouthful of food on his plate. "The very first town we come to, let's go to the bank there and ask to see its president. He'll be sure to know father. We'll tell him all about this money and have him put it in his bank—in escrow it's called—and then have him send word to the police or the courts or whoever it is they have to send word to. That'll put it out of our hands. What do you say?"

"Fine!" assented Abel in relief. "And till then don't let's look at the bag any oftener than we have to, hey? I don't want to get all sore inside, thinkin' about that tractor and the ten-acre corner."

"All right. We'll do just that. But," Don hesitated, "there's one more thing we ought to do, before we put the bag out of sight for good. If money is in escrow, they have to know just how much of it there is. And —"

"We know, all right!" grumbled Abel. "We counted it careful enough. It was —"

"We counted the rolls we poured out of the bag," assented Don. "But there were pockets or compartments or something like that, in the sides of the bag. Perhaps there's more money in the pockets. Or"—with a return of movie memories—"or papers."

"You look, then," said Abel crossly. "I just told you I'm no measly saint. I'm sick of countin' cash that my bum conscience won't let me keep."

Donald went to the lean-to, returning with the bag which he set down on the floor. As he opened it, Abel turned his back and scowled out over the turbulent waste of waters.

"We ought to learn to do the way father says a bank cashier or a teller has to," Donald was saying as he brought out the bag and opened it. "Father says a bank employee is worthless and untrustworthy till he forgets that money is money and looks at it only as counters in the finance game he is playing. Father says—"

He came to an abrupt halt in his homily. As he talked, Don had removed the packages of bills methodically from the satchel. Next he had thrust an exploring hand into the right-side pocket in the lining. The hand came out empty and dived into the left pocket. It was then that Don had checked his discourse, for he drew forth a knotted and dirty handkerchief which contained something more or less bulky.

Don untied the hasty knot which held the handkerchief's four corners together, bag-fashion. There in his palm, nestling among the handkerchief folds, lay his stolen watch and wallet!

Gurgling with bewildered joy, Don opened the wallet and pulled out the money therein. Not a bill had been taken.

A queer glint of scared gravity crept into Abel's jubilant eyes.

"Say!" he breathed. "D'you notice we never got back that cash and that grand watch of yours till after we made up our minds to play honest about the rest of the money?"

"There's something else that just popped into my head, while I was opening the bag," said Don, later, when the satchel had been hidden away once more in the lean-to. "When a big sum of money like that is returned to the losers, there's almost always a good-sized reward paid to the finder. That reward will be yours, Abe. I've got my share," tapping the vest wherein the watch and wallet once more reposed.

"Huh!" muttered Abel ungraciously, albeit he thrilled at the idea. "We'll wait till we see the reward before we squabble about dividin' it."

Simon Peter broke in on his master's grumblings in a truly dramatic way. For some minutes the collie had been sniffing the air worriedly, straining his eyes in an effort to look upstream.

Now, with a bark that was more like a cry of mingled fear and fury, he leaped up and made a fierce dash to the edge of the raft, flinging his big furry body between the water and the boys he loved. He stood as though to shield them from some peril, crouching low, every hair abristle, his lips curled back from his terrible white teeth, his massive throat thunderous with a ceaseless succession of murderous growls.

Both boys jumped to their feet. Then a simultaneous gasp of horror broke from their parted lips. Instinctively they caught hold of each other for protection and, with blanched faces and terror-stricken eyes, peered above them at something that was approaching, with deadly directness of motion, through the tossing yellow waters.

Now they understood the note of ill-conquered fear in the growl of the gallant dog who had flung himself between them and the fast approaching horror.

# Chapter VII

TOWARD the raft was moving swiftly a V-shaped wave, as the tawny waters parted to make way for the swimmer.

The apex of the wave was a dark triangular head, well-nigh as large as the collie's own—an evil and glistening head, with tiny and lidless beadlike eyes.

Behind the evil head, at intervals above the surface of the river, arose thick, dark, undulating coils, that appeared and vanished alternately, with the motion of swimming.

The oncoming monster was a snake. Yet surely, since the prehistoric ages, no such serpent had ever before swum the Mississippi River. As well as the deceptive glimpses of the creature could show, as its coils appeared and reappeared through the yellow water, the snake was fully twenty-five feet in length with a body as thick in places as a man's thigh.

Abel Herrick stared, thunderstruck. He had never seen nor heard of a snake like this. He doubted the evidence of his own bulging eyes.

"It's—it's the python from the circus at the fair!" jabbered Donald, shivering from head to heel. "I saw it there. It must have been swept away in the flood. It—"

His words were drowned in a fanfare of mad barking from the collie. Simon Peter had decided to try to frighten away the dreadful foe which apparently was not to be checked by the dog's menacing attitude. But the serpent did not seem to heed the fearful din. On it came, straight as an arrow, toward the raft. Its undulating body seemed to take on new speed as it neared the table edge where crouched the valiant dog.

Simon Peter ceased his useless racket. For an instant he quivered as with palsy and cast a swift glance of appeal at his human gods who stood terror-stricken in the raft's center. Then, seeming to realize that it was he who must defend them and that they could offer no aid, he whimpered softly, braced himself and stood his ground, head lowered, teeth bared—tense, heroic.

A dog has instinctive fear of a big snake. Fear was fighting for mastery in the collie's heart. Great was that fear. But greater was his love for the two panic-smitten boys behind him. Wherefore the collie braced himself for battle with a hideous foe which he knew was his superior in prowess.

On rushed the monster through the water. It was long since the python had fed. The tumbling journey down the river had tired and chilled and infuriated it. Here in sight was warmth, in the shape of the fire—snakes love fire as much as do cats. Here, too, was food, as scent and sight told the python. A seventy-pound collie was a most desirable meal in the snake's empty and chilled condition. Also, there were other living and eatable things aboard the raft. Rage seconded hunger in the glint of its lidless eyes at sight of the foolishly threatening dog in its path.

While its nose was still ten feet away from the table edge, the python halted, churning the water to foam as it coiled. Up in air arose the awful three-cornered head, as two yards of neck protruded from the river's surface.

Then it struck.

The lower body clove the waves in its forward surge. The high-held head snapped forward like a whiplash. The cruel jaws parted to an incredible wideness revealing crooked yellow fangs and a vast expanse of pink-yellow throat.

Now, a python is perhaps the swiftest-moving creature in existence at close quarters, when hunger or rage stirs it from its wonted lethargy. It strikes with a speed that the eye cannot follow. In its native jungle or even in ordinary captivity, this snake would have flashed past the collie's puny guard and have had the dog helpless in a single stroke of the fearsome head.

But for five endless years this python had dwelt in a traveling circus, in cramped quarters, jostled about on innumerable trains. No such luxurious life had it led as is meted out to its brethren in stationary zoos. The snake's unbelievable strength had been sapped by this long course of ill-treatment. Nor had the past three days of almost perpetual immersion in cold and tossing waters improved its condition any more than they had improved its demoniac temper.

Still deadly and a terrible foe for any brute or any human to encounter, it had, none the less, lost some of the speed that was its chief reliance.

Down flashed the yawning-jawed triangular head, straight for the snarling collie. But when the jaws smote the deck where Simon Peter's braced feet had just stood the dog was no longer there.

Springing aside, with only the very barest fraction of a second to spare, Simon Peter had eluded the lightning-swift stroke by a margin of perhaps half an inch. As he dodged, the collie slashed with his curving white eyeteeth.

A collie is nearer to his ancestor, the wolf, than is any other domesticated dog. He has lost the wolf's savage heart, but he has retained the wolf's uncannily resourceful brain, as well as the wolf's elusive prowess, in battle. A collie does not seek a certain hold and hang on, as do the bulldog and the bulldog's cousin, the Airedale. He flashes in and out, biting, slashing, dodging, feinting, snapping at a dozen spots in as many seconds. He is not a pleasant opponent.

Simon Peter eluded the python's lunge and slashed ferociously at the darting head as it whizzed past him. The python jerked its head back from the futile lunge. In its slimy dark neck was a deep furrow, where the collie's eyetooth had shorn a gash from which flowed a little river of blood. The dog had won the first round of the pitifully unequal battle. He braced himself for a renewal of the snake's attack.

All sign of fear was gone from Simon Peter. Defiantly, almost gaily, he awaited the monster's next move. His plumy tail swung rhythmically. His deepset eyes were ablaze.

Lashing the water, in pain from the ragged rent in its neck, the python flung its ugly head aloft and struck again with the same bewildering speed, half blind with fury at the failure of the first assault.

A second time the collie failed to remain in the spot where the snake expected to find him. Eluding the darted fangs by even less margin than before, the dog slipped to one side with eel-like quickness, and the fierce white teeth drove into the throat of the python from the left side until they almost met.

The jerky withdrawal of the wounded neck lifted Simon Peter clean off his feet and some distance in air, before he could reopen his powerfully grinding jaws. The dog fell to the deck in a furry heap, the breath knocked out of him by the drop.

But on the instant he was up again and on the alert. This time there was scope for him to regain his lost breath. For the python was thrashing madly about in the river, churning the yellow water to foam, swinging its wounded neck to and fro high above the surface as though in an attempt to shake off the torturing pain.

Twice it made as though to return to the charge, but both times sheered away at sight of the challenging dog.

Then the writhing coils relaxed. The huge body sank limply under the water, head and all, a shadowy bulk showing momentarily, just beneath the roiled surface.

The entire fight had scarcely lasted a minute. Not long enough for the two boys to rouse from their paralysis of fright at the incredible apparition. Now, with a gasp, they relaxed. Abel flung his arms about the victorious collie in a bear-hug. Don, unnerved, stammered:

"Simon Peter! You're the heroest dog, ever! And we stood by like cowards and let you fight for us. Oh, I'm—!"

Don got no further. With a wrench, the collie tore himself free from Abel's embrace, sprang clean over the kneeling boy and hurled himself across the twenty-two-foot expanse of raft to the edge opposite the scene of conflict.

As the lads' perplexed gaze followed this odd maneuver, they were just in time to see something shaped like a gigantic black arrowhead— something which reared itself against the raft edge from out the depths of the river—at which the collie was flying in a delirium of war lust.

They understood. The first glimpse of the evil three-cornered head told them the python had not been beaten off, but had merely shifted the attack after the consummate cunning of its kind.

It had dived beneath the raft to the far side and had come to the surface, this time at not a distance of ten feet, but so close that its horny nose rubbed the table edge. With slithering haste it was crawling aboard.

By the time Simon Peter's bound had carried him across the deck, the python's head and some seven feet or more of its glittering length were on the raft. At the dog's onset, the python flung forward to meet him, the lunge bringing another yard of its slimy body on deck.

Almost in mid-air Simon Peter swerved in his furious charge. Neither boy could note the collie's lightning motion in avoiding the striking head. But they saw the python's wide mouth graze the dog's left shoulder in passing. They saw the compact furry catapult swing to the left, even as he felt the grazing touch. In what seemed to be the same move Simon Peter's jaws found their goal in the serpent's momentarily exposed throat.

Up reared the python, hissing and coiling. This time the collie did not loose his hold as his feet left the ground. Realizing that he had found a vital spot, he hung on, his mighty jaws grinding deep and deeper. Down crashed the snake's head and forebody to the verge of the deck. At last, the python had a steady fulcrum for his deadly leverage.

Before the dog could let go or spring aside, a thick coil had been whirled round him. Simon Peter must have known the fight was lost and that the first real constriction of the resistless coil would crush him to pulp. But he did not loose his grip nor cease to grind the curved eye-teeth farther and farther into his foe's throat.

He merely hurled his own body to one side as far as the coil would permit toward the water. The weight of his seventy pounds and the erratic sideways fling of that weight, overset the python's precarious balance on the raft's slippery edge. With a loud splash, dog and snake rolled overboard and sank, close-locked, beneath the water.

They vanished from sight just as Abel had recovered enough of his shattered self-control to snatch up one of the two long and heavy boat poles. Don, at his example, swung aloft the other pole.

But there was nothing on which to vent their new-found valor. The dog had rid them of their enemy, but he himself was somewhere far below the surface, strangling in a coil of the dying snake.

A sob broke from Don. As if the sob were a signal, something black and shiny burst its way into view through and above the current. It was an arc of one of the python's coils. It came into sight a bare yard away from the raft, arching well above the surface, as though the python were still struggling down there to rid itself of the drowning collie's throat grip or to tighten its coil and thus kill its opponent outright.

As the section of the scaly body appeared both boys brought down their heavy boat poles upon it with all their force and weight.

With a double thwack the big poles descended. In another moment they crashed down upon the snake once again. Then, all at once, the whole river for a radius of thirty feet appeared to be undergoing a volcanic upheaval.

Like other snakes, a python is most vulnerable in his sinuous but never well-protected spine. Break the back of a snake and he is as good as dead.

Impotent, in death agony, the giant snake thrashed about in the river, alongside the raft.

The boys scarcely noticed the monster's death throes, for at the very first convulsion of the tossing body a half-drowned dog had been shot into the air. Two loving sets of arms were reaching for the exhausted Simon Peter and lifting him aboard. The collie had fought the good fight. He was still alive, with no bones broken, although he was deathly sick.

Here somewhere in the bottom of the Mississippi's mud lie the remains of one of the largest and costliest pythons ever imported into the United States. Snared in its native Indian jungle and for years the star attraction of its owner's show, it met death at the last in battle with a mere dog reenforced by two fourteen-year-old boys.

Leaving the fatigued dog dozing by the blaze, Don and Abel proceeded to make their belated exploration of the scrap-heap island. Nine-tenths of its contents were less than worthless to the young explorers. But there remained enough to pile the raft's center with food and fuel and to patch the lean-to and furnish the voyagers with two rickety chairs and a fair quantity of drenched bedding.

Also to give them a strong and serviceable little rowboat and three mismated oars, to say nothing of some fifty feet of rope.

But the cream of the collection was found by Don under a bumpy blanket of piled-up river refuse. This find was a garishly painted eighteen-foot picnic boat, crumpled up as to bow and with a gaping hole stove into its side amidships. Fastened to its ample stern was a detachable boat motor, which had apparently been powerful enough to send the two-hundred-pound picnic wherry along at a fair clip. The motor and its rudder attachment had escaped injury in the various flood collisions which had destroyed the boat itself.

Don fell upon this bit of treasure with a squeal of bliss. He was a born lover of machinery. His own motor boat until its smash in the rapids below Mitch Dawes' had been the joy of his heart.

With Abel's inexpert help, Don detached the motor and rudder from the crippled wherry and between them they lugged the heavy machine aboard the raft. There Don insisted on attaching it to one edge of the table—a tolerably easy feat, as the motor was constructed for such changes of base.

"There we are!" he exclaimed as he stood back to survey his work. "Now we've got motive power and steering for our raft! After this she won't go blundering along like a drunken top, bunting into everything. I don't suppose this engine can drive such a clumsy thing at any rate of speed. But she'll have steering way and a mile or two an hour of speed apart from the current. We—"

"I see," said Abel. "But are these gasoline motors geared so's to run without gasoline? 'Cause, if they ain't, I don't know what good this will do us."

"Come on!" Don exhorted. "There's everything else in this tree-top junk yard. And there's pretty sure to be gas here too. We've run across lots of boat-yard truck and things from riverside garages. We're due to strike gas if we look hard enough."

An hour's rummaging search and the prying up of roof edges and the knocking open of floating boxes gave them what they sought. Here a little in a wallowing barrel, there a little more in ten-gallon tins that had been too nearly empty to sink, once in a half-full thirty-gallon cask and again in a full five-gallon can that had been stored in a tool box too big for the tin's weight to sink it, they found gasoline. They found enough to fill almost to the brim a water-tight barrel they rolled aboard the raft. They found enough motor oil, too, to fill one of the big tins.

"You see," triumphed Don, as the last of the engine fuel was in place. "We've got our engine and our steering gear. And we've got enough gas and oil to run them as far as Annsburg, anyhow. What do you think of—"

"I think," replied Abel—"I think it's Elijah's chariot of fire, comin' to take we-uns up to heaven!"

Abel's eyes and Abel's mind were fixed upon the river. Don followed the other's rapt gaze.

"A chariot of fire!" babbled Abel, shading his eyes from a glare of light that hurt them. "A-comin' to snatch us to heaven. Gee!"

# Chapter VIII

ABEL HERRICK'S phrase, a chariot of fire, was perhaps the best possible description of the object on which the boys riveted their eyes.

Down the river, shoved slowly along by the current, it came, the whirlpool eddy drawing it steadily toward the raft. It was perhaps a hundred yards away when Abel's amazed exclamation drew his chum's attention to it.

The thing was hard to describe. Roughly, it resembled a wheelless triumphal car that might have been transported bodily from ancient Rome. About fifteen feet long and five feet wide, it was covered with chasing and with scores of embossed figures of weird shape and posture. At either end it rode high above the water. On the front rose the figure of a giant mermaid.

The whole chariot was bright gold in color—mermaid and carven figures and all. The sunlight poured down upon it, turning its gilded surface to the hue of molten fire. The thing blazed and glittered in the sun as though it were swathed in living flame.

To add to the wonder and the rank impossibility of such a chariot's presence on the face of the respectable twentieth-century Mississippi River, some living creature was swaggering drunkenly from end to end of it.

As well as they could, through the fierce glitter of the gilded chariot, the boys tried to focus their dazzled gaze on this ever-moving passenger. As the golden chariot swung closer to them, they were able to make out most of its details.

At first glance it seemed to them the chariot's occupant was a gigantic and ludicrously fat man, clad in a balloon like suit of bedraggled red, white and blue. At times the giant walked erect with a waddling and rolling gait, again it dropped to all fours and scrambled along the roof of the chariot like a monstrous cat. Once it rose to its full height and stretched out a pair of fat and tricolored arms toward the raft, as though ordering an invisible helmsman to steer toward it.

"We—we can't really be seeing this!" whispered Donald Page. "There isn't any such sight on earth. What's—what's that man trying to do? And what man ever looked like that? He—"

Then, as a swing of the current pushed the chariot more rapidly toward

them, the sun went under a cloud and the boys could see with more
distinctness. The mystery of the monstrous and grotesque red-white-
and-blue figure ceased to be a mystery and became a grim reality.

The wearer of the gaudy attire was not a gigantic man. Nor was he
wearing that ridiculous costume through choice. He was a tremendous
black bear. Like the python, he was evidently a member of the fair circus.
Still incased in the costume wherein he had been made to perform his
clumsy tricks, the bear had struck out for the nearest floating thing that
would hold his weight. This was when the wave had dumped him and the
circus and the whole Wyckoff fair into the Mississippi River.

The object he had climbed aboard was one of the gorgeous street-
parade wagons of the circus. Its wheels and floor and lower portion were
under water, but its gilded and embellished upper half still rode the flood
with wabbly majesty.

The bear had sighted the raft and the boys. Perhaps the aroma of
cooked chicken was alluring to him and stirred his starving stomach to
new life. At all events, as the chariot of fire rolled near and nearer to the
raft, bruin crouched at its gilded edge, teeth aglint, muscles tensed for the
bound which should carry him aboard.

He was not a pretty sight nor, for all his comic trappings, was there
now anything laughable about the huge body that quivered for a spring.

If the python had petrified the boys into moveless horror, this new
enemy did not. There was something tangible and normal about a bear—
an absence of the gruesome fear which a serpent inspires. Moreover, they
were not to be scared into helplessness a second time by any peril. They
were too much ashamed of their recent inaction for that.

Picking up his knife which still lay open beside his plate, Abel cut franti-
cally at the rope which moored the raft to the pine top. As the last frayed
strand parted, he caught up one of the two boat poles and thrust with all
his might against the swaying bank of wreckage.

But the pressure of the current was strong. A tangle of river jetsam had
already begun to fasten the raft to the rest of the island. For a moment
or two Abel thrust in vain. He called to Don to come to his aid in getting
the table out into the stream and away from the path of the approaching
chariot.

Abel turned as he called. He turned to see that an eddy had whirled the
chariot several yards nearer and that there could be no possible chance

of pushing the raft free before the gilded hulk would pass within jumping distance of them. He swung aloft his pole and faced the oncoming danger. His mouth was very dry and his palms were very wet, but his arms were steady and his belligerent gaze did not shrink.

Meantime, Simon Peter had been roused from his sleep of exhaustion by the turmoil about him. The dog lifted his tired head lazily. Then eye and nostril alike told him of the new peril. Fatigue forgotten, the collie was on his feet in one bound, at the verge of the raft, growling and ready for battle.

"No, you don't!" declared Don, thrusting the eager dog aside. "You're not going to do all the work again. You're all in, as it is. Here's the time we fight for you, old chap, not you for us!"

As he spoke, Don snatched up a blazing brand from the fire. In the back of his brain was a vague memory of reading that wild animals dread flame. Wherefore he brandished the fiery billet of pitch pine in the very face of the bear. The result was anything but what he had expected.

The chariot was a bare eight feet from the raft. Bruin, his teeth bared and his little red eyes fierce, was crouching for the spring that should land him among his puny foes and within reach of the food he craved.

Then before his hungrily warlike visage was whirled a firebrand. So near that the heat stung him and the glare dazzled him, the flaming torch was shaken. The bear's tense posture relaxed. He sheathed his saberlike claws. The light of battle died in the red eyes.

Slowly and with solemn dignity bruin rose to his full height, his tattered tricolor garments flapping noisily round him in the breeze. Tucking his forefeet close up under his chin and with his long black snout pointing piously heavenward, he began to dance.

Both boys gasped aloud in sheer amaze. Then, from reaction, they burst into a fit of hysterical laughter. A moment earlier they had been braced for a death fight with a murderous wild beast. And, lo! This man-eating monster was seeking to entertain them with a circus dance! Small wonder the relief turned them weak and hysterical!

Simon Peter alone did not cease his sharp vigilance, but crouched, alert and wrathful, waiting for the queerly postponed onset. Don lowered his blazing brand, then at once began to wave it again as vigorously as before at the dancing brute.

"I get the idea!" he shouted to Abel, choking back his laughter and continuing to brandish the torch. "I've read how they train bears. They do it by torture just as father says all animal acts are trained. They put the bear on hot iron to make him dance, at first. After that the sight of fire reminds him to dance. If he doesn't, he's burned till it does. This bear is dancing because he thinks we'll burn him if he doesn't. Father says every trained animal in a show has been tortured into—"

"Well, he won't dance all day!" broke in the more practical Abel, picking up his boat pole again. "When he finds we keep our distance, he'll stop keeping his. Just go on waving that burning stick at him while I pry us loose!"

Abel fell to his task with the pole once more, and now that he was cooler he substituted skill for panic force, in his effort to ease the raft off the island's margin. With a final twist and shove, aided this time by a new swirl of the eccentric current, he pushed the table free.

Don tossed the firebrand aboard the chariot, which was all but grating against the raft. Then he seized the other boat pole. The burning wood fell at the bear's ploddingly dancing feet. Bruin abandoned his dance and retreated to the farther end of the chariot, where he cowered, whimpering.

The boys worked like mad with their poles, thrusting clear of the island and out into the main current.

As they worked they saw the chariot come to a halt in the very niche of floating shore that their table had just occupied. They saw the bear make a cringing detour of the smoking brand and scramble ashore. After a scared glance toward the departing craft, he began to climb to a roof side where Abel had left the entrails and heads of two butchered chickens and a number of half-rotted apples.

"Good old bear!" observed Don. "I'm glad he got safe ashore and I'm glad there's enough food on the island to make him as fat as butter. I've taken a liking to the poor tortured beast. He danced so pathetically! When the flood goes down I hope he can make his way to the hills before the circus people catch him again. How about it? Shall we work round to the other side and anchor off the lower end of the island? I doubt if he could climb over all that wreckage on the ridge and get at us there."

Abel paused in his strenuous task of poling and let the raft bowl clumsily downstream, past the tree-top collection of flotsam. With portentous sternness he spoke.

"We've got enough truck aboard," said he, "to feed and warm us for a week. And that motor thing will keep us steered and give us headway—if it works out like you say it will. And we've got a dinghy in tow—a dinghy with oars. But even if we was driftin' on a log, without anything to eat, I'd say: 'Let's we go on a-driftin', indefinite, sooner'n go back to that island!'

"I'd say it good and loud. We got grub and a passel of other good truck off'n that island. But, likewise, we got snarled up suthin' turrible with a pizen sarpent and a big he-walloper of a bear. And if a bear and a snake c'n land there from the circus, then there's no reason why other snakes and bears can't land there from the same circus. Not to mention lions and tigers and hippopotamuses and sich.

"Two varmints landed there inside of two hours. What's to keep the whole menagerie from bringin' up there durin' the next two days? Hey? Tell me that! I wouldn't go back there again for the best fifty acres of bottom land on the Mississip'. No, sir, we're a-goin' on and we're goin' to keep on a-goin', if I've got any vote in this yer meetin'. We're a-goin' till we're as far from that pesky island as we c'n git."

"Good!" assented Don. "That's the way I felt too. Only I was afraid you'd guy me for being afraid. There was too much excitement there to suit me. Reach me that oil can, will you?" he ended, kneeling beside the motor.

A few minutes of fairly skillful work on Don's part evoked a cough from the engine, then another and then a whirring. The propeller churned up the water to white foam. The raft shivered, steadied and began to move slowly forward with a steadier motion than the current had imparted. A very respectable wake stretched out astern. The raft was progressing under her own power. For the first time, probably, in aquatic history, a motor table was sailing the stream.

Don was wildly elated. He waxed more and more jubilant as the table responded, though sluggishly, to his rudder's commands. Even Abel felt a thrill of pride in their queer craft's new accomplishment. Watching his chum's dawning enthusiasm, Don ventured to take advantage of it.

"Back on the island there," he began cautiously, "I started to tell you about a plan I had. Then, before I could do it, that python butted in on us. Like to hear it now?"

"Sure," assented Abel, with more civility than real interest.

"Of course," explained Don, "it's pretty selfish of me. And if you don't like it, just say so and we'll let it drop. I told you how crazy my father is about this table. He'll be sore all over if it's lost, after all the time and thought and cash he's spent in getting it and having it shipped from California and after the way the Annsburg papers wrote it up and everything. If we desert it or get taken off by a search party, the poor old table will go drifting down to the Gulf or into some bayou and get lost forever. Or some roustabout will find it on a sand bar and chop it up for firewood. At best, if some tug gets hold of it, there'll be a whopping salvage bill to pay, if father wants it back. So I was wondering—especially since we got this motor—I was wondering—"

"You was wonderin'," supplemented Abel as Don hesitated. "You was awonderin' why it wouldn't be a whoppin' and plumb dandy scheme for us to run this-yer table all the way downstream to Annsburg, moor it there and waltz up to your dad and tell him: 'Daddy, here's you-all's fine big table, all safe and sound. It'll need to have its top planed a wee peckle and repolished up. But it's all here, dad.' That's what you're chewin' over, Donny. And you're scared it won't make a hit with me. Well, I'm here to tell you it's a corkin' good idee and you c'n count me in on it. I—"

"Oh, Abe, you're a brick!" exploded the much-relieved Don, pump-handling the grinning youth. "I want to take it home so much! And I was sure you'd kick and want us to get ashore at the first town we could reach. Thanks, ever so much, Abe! You're—"

"Aw, shucks!" the embarrassed Abel interrupted him. "Don't go makin' a song about it! It'll be first-rate sport. And it'll save car fare home. And, well, this-yer table's kept us alive for quite a spell, now. 'Twouldn't reely be square to turn her adrift. We-all can't be many miles north of Annsburg. And the flood's sinkin' every hour. See, there's bumpy hills and trees and things over yonder, that was all under water yest'd'y. We'd ought to be able to git our bearin's from some land-mark pretty soon now."

"And first town we can touch at," chimed in Don, "we'll stop and deposit that bag in the bank there, the way we agreed to. We've got no right to risk keeping it, in case of an upset or something. We'll deposit it and we'll send a telegram to our home people and then start on for Annsburg, aboard the good ship Directors' Table. This is better than all the movies I ever went to. It's as good as a cruise in a treasure-island ship. We'll elect Simon Peter for captain of our galleon; you and I'll take turns being first mate."

"If it hadn't been for Simon Peter," said Abel, rumpling the collie's soft ears, "we'd be at the bottom of the Mississip', somewhere upstream."

All the rest of the day they drifted, the motor turned on only part of the time, when steering headway was needed. That night they tied up to a tree top. Don wisely left several yards of slack in their mooring rope. In the morning the rope was all but taut, so fast was the flood receding.

The voyagers slept late from the preceding day's fatigue and it was almost noon when they cast off from the tree and resumed their downstream journey.

At dusk the lights of a town glowed forth as the raft neared a jutting point of land. Thither Don steered. Before darkness fell he was able to recognize a double spire and to know from it that they were approaching Gattysville, some fifteen miles north of Annsburg.

Night had settled down when Don brought the awkward raft cleverly to a stop at a deep nick in the shore line. The nick was formed by a street that ran up from the river to the center of town.

The boys tied the raft to an iron knob which proved to be a half-submerged hitching post. Then with Simon Peter at their heels they started up the street. Don carried the bag tightly in his right hand.

Presently they came to the railroad station. Entering, they told the drowsy clerk they wanted to send two telegrams. The clerk yawned and replied that a lot of people wanted to do the same thing, but that all wires were still down. Don next asked the name of the local bank president and where he lived.

"Colonel Branch is pres'd'nt of the First National," answered the clerk. "I don't know where he lives, but I've seen him sometimes in the lobby of the Lee Hotel, this time of evening."

The boys set off for the hotel. Incidentally they set off for an adventure quite as perilous in its own way as had been their encounter with the python.

# Chapter IX

UP THE steep street plodded the two adventurers, Don still clutching the black bag of treasure, Abel close beside him.

Simon Peter frisked gayly about them, rejoicing in this first chance in days for exercise. He explored every dark passageway, he stared into every front yard. Once he picked up a stick and trotted eagerly over to the boys, pausing in front of each in turn, mutely inviting them to throw the stick he had found and thus to let him show off his skill at retrieving.

But they were too absorbed in their errand to have thought for the collie.

"We'll ask at the desk," Don was explaining, "for Colonel Branch. If he's there we'll ask to see him alone for a few minutes. I'll mention my father's name and I know he'll have heard of him. Then we'll just tell him our story and turn the bag over to him and get a receipt for it. That will finish our share of the business. We can sleep at the hotel, if you like, and start the raft for Annsburg at daybreak. We ought to get there before night, even against such cross-currents as have been bothering us all day. It'll be nice to sleep in a real bed again, won't it, and to eat a hotel supper?"

"It'll be a heap nicer to get rid of this measly treasure bag," said Abel. "Now that we can't have the money, I've begun to hate it. I wish Mister Claude C. Desmond had—"

"Here's the Lee Hotel," interrupted Don, pausing at the foot of a low flight of stone steps leading up to a house with an illuminated sign above the door. "Come along, Simon Peter! Drop that stick and come on in."

The hotel lobby was small and dingy. It smelt of dead dinners, the odor of cabbage predominating. It was hazy from the smoke of many cigars, some of them so rank as to set Simon Peter to sneezing. A dozen men were lounging there, some leaning against the desk and chatting, others tilted back in chairs against the discolored wall.

Don and Abel made their way to the desk.

"We would like to speak to Colonel Branch," said Don to an obese man who lolled behind the cigar counter.

"All right, sonny," replied the fat man, eying the two with amused interest and casting an appraising glance over the collie that stood statuelike beside Abel. "All right, speak to him all you want to. Nobody'll stop you."

"Is he here?" asked Abel, forestalling a less mild retort from Don, who had flushed hotly at the man's banter.

"Well, he isn't concealed anywhere about me," drawled the fat humorist.

"Colonel Branch will be wantin' to see us," said Abel stoutly, as he met the man's grin. "My friend here is the son of his side partner, the pres'd'nt of the Annsburg bank. Where c'n we find him, please?"

"He was in here a while ago," was the answer, more civil this time. "He said he had some work to do, so he was going home. He lives on Beauregard Street—street just back of this. About two squares toward the river. Big reddish-brick house with a cup'la onto it. You can't miss it. Not unless the river riz again since dark and washed it away."

"Can we get a room here for the night?" asked Don, mentally noting the directions for finding the bank president's home. "When we come from Colonel Branch's we'd like to——"

A sharp tug at his sleeve drew Don's attention toward Abel and broke short his speech. The country boy's eyes had been roving interestedly round the hotel lobby—almost the first he had ever been in—for the past few seconds. Now, his mouth set and his hand trembling, he was drawing his chum toward the door in rough haste.

For a fraction of a second Don hung back, then, noting Abel's stark eagerness, he suffered himself to be led along. The desk was near the door and in three steps the two lads were out on the shallow veranda.

"What's up?" demanded Don, somewhat annoyed by the other's abruptness and air of mystery. "Why did you——"

"Come along!" ordered Abel, whistling to Simon Peter and running down the steps.

Nor did he pause until he had rounded the first corner and was standing in the shadow of the ill-lit cross street. There the wondering Don caught up with him.

"Did you see who was sittin' just behind us while we was talkin' to that man?" asked Abel, his voice shaky with excitement. "Did you see who was sittin' there, jawin' with a couple of other city fellers? He quit jawin', though, when he seen us, and he kind of slunk behind the corner of the desk. I got a glimpse of him just as he saw us. So I gave you the tip to git out."

"I don't understand," said Don, puzzled. "Who was——"

"It was that Desmond chap!" exclaimed Abel, "sittin' there as cool as——"

"No!" cried Don in amaze. "Why, Desmond is drowned. He——"

"Maybe he is," grunted Abel. "And then again maybe he ain't. Anyways, there he was a-settin'. He seen us. And he knowed us. I c'd tell that. And

I seen his eyes bug out when they lit onto that bag. But he never made a move to git up and claim it. That means it's stolen cash and he dassen't ask us for it. He hid back so's we wouldn't rec'nize him too. That ain't the way a square man'd act when he had a chance to git back all that cash, is it? So I yanked you out of there. I'm thinkin' the sooner we turn this bag over to the bank pres'd'nt, the better it'll be all round. Desmond's likely to git after us, if he c'n catch us alone. And them fellers he was chinnin' with may be in cahoots with him. Come along!"

Paying no heed to Don's volley of questions and suppositions, Abel led the way toward the next intersecting street—the street whereon they had been told Colonel Branch lived. Don kept pace with him and the dog trotted happily ahead. Simon Peter could tell from the agitation of his two masters that some excitement was afoot. And he had all of a collie's inborn love for excitement.

Turning the corner, they started down Beauregard Street, trying, in the dim light, to make out a red-brick house with a cupola. The town's electric lighting system had been paralyzed by the flood. This residence thoroughfare was in almost total darkness.

"I'll ask at the next house," said Don, "if the colonel lives this side of—"

Out of the darkness behind them shot an arm and the bag was wrenched from the unsuspecting boy's grasp.

In practically the same motion the highwayman's other hand smote Don athwart the side of the head with a force that lifted the luckless lad clean off the sidewalk and landed him on his back in the muddy gutter. Abel, wheeling about at the sound, was neatly tripped up before he could get a fair look at the shadowy form that had crept upon them out of the darkness.

He caught at the air to balance himself, then sprawled on all fours. As he rose to his feet he saw someone running away at top speed and heard the light thud of the fugitive's receding feet. All this in the merest three seconds from the time when first the hand seized the loosely guarded bag.

Abel scrambled up as quickly as might be. So did the more heavily thrown Don. Yet neither of them had the remotest chance of overhauling the swift-running man, even if they could have prevailed against him when caught. Nevertheless, he was pursued, and pursued at lightning speed, before either boy was able to collect enough presence of mind to shout for help.

Through the darkness something whizzed past the bemused lads—something silent, furry, furious—something that had been trotting unconcernedly along in front of them when they were attacked and had turned as the man struck, taking in the situation at a glance.

The sight of his two deities' overthrow had sent a blaze of righteous rage to Simon Peter's brain. Many a dog will fly at any man who assails his master, but Simon Peter had also caught this man's scent. The scent was familiar to the collie as that of the foe who had once boarded the raft and had sought to stab him. This memory lent speed to the dog's scurrying feet.

By the time Desmond had fairly gotten into his stride, holding the bag against his chest with both hands as a football player might hug the pigskin, the dog was close at his heels.

Few animals, and no humans, can equal the speed of a young collie. In a second or so Simon Peter was within a yard of Desmond's straining form. He forbore to drive for the leg or ankle, as was his instinct. He realized that this was an enemy to be pulled down, not merely to be hurt.

Wherefore, gathering all his strength and incredible speed, the dog launched himself through the air, rising to thrice his own height as he sprang.

Desmond, in full flight, suddenly felt a weight of seventy pounds crash against his back between the shoulder blades.

The balance of a runner is always precarious in the extreme, as is shown by the fact that a slight stumble will almost invariably pitch him headlong to the ground—a stumble that would scarcely break the stride of a man who is merely walking.

One foot clear off the ground and the other foot rising on its toe tip for the next step, Desmond received the furry catapult between his shoulders.

Under that unexpected impact his body shot forward regardless of his legs. He pitched downward, throwing out his arms by age-old instinct to steady himself, forgetting the precious burden he was carrying close to his breast.

Down he went, his own momentum lending speed to his fall. His right wrist struck the pavement first, doubling over with a force that snapped two of its bones. Next his chin came into contact with the ground. The violence of his fall had been broken somewhat in the breaking of his wrist. This probably saved him from a broken neck as well.

As it was, the smiting of his jaw against the pavement had the same effect on the man as might a tremendous fist blow on the point of the chin. His muscles sagged and he lay unconscious and moveless.

But Simon Peter had not paused to note the effect of the tumble on his victim. Whining in fierce eagerness, the dog was seeking to burrow into the crumpled mass of clothing and flesh, to find the throat hold he craved.

He was searching thus for the throat when Abel and Don came up at a staggering run and pulled the collie back from the senseless thief.

"He's killed him!" babbled Abel in awe, as they bent over the man. "He's—"

A shudder and a stifled groan from Desmond set at rest the boy's first dread. He groped for a match and struck it, while Don still held the growling collie by the ruff. The tiny flare of light revealed to him the familiar face of the fog-disperser genius. It revealed this and something else to Don—something that lay on the narrow sidewalk a few feet in front of the victim. Don let go of the dog and made a dive for the thing he had caught sight of in the match flare.

"Abe!" he whispered wildly. "Here's the bag! I've got it. Is he really dead?"

"Dead, nuthin'!" returned Abel, a little ashamed of his own brief scare. "He's beginnin' to twitch and mumble. In another minute he'll be alive and after us again. And them men that was talkin' with him, they're maybe after us too, Come on! Let's run for it!"

On common impulse they turned and scuttled down the dark street as fast as their tired legs would carry them.

Simon Peter looked down longingly at the prone body of his enemy, snarling as he noted the man's gradual return toward consciousness. Then with much reluctance the dog followed the mandates of duty and cantered down the street in the wake of his scampering masters.

For perhaps a quarter of a mile the lads fled, side by side, pausing only to skirt such obstacles as chanced to be in their path. To their frightened senses, Desmond and a million fellow desperadoes seemed to be racing after them, scarce a stride behind.

They forgot to resume their search for the red-brick house with a cupola. They forgot everything except the terrific need of getting themselves as far as possible away from the man who had attacked them, the man who, but for Simon Peter, would by now be safely hidden somewhere with the recovered bag of money.

Then, as they neared the river, Abel's brain began to function more clearly as fatigue and exercise cooled it. If, indeed, Desmond or any of his confederates were chasing them, the two would presently be cornered at the water's edge. It would take two or three minutes to untie and cast off the raft. In that time, their pursuers might readily capture them and the bag, even the valued table itself.

Spurting, Abel caught up with Don whose longer legs had gradually carried him some yards ahead.

"Duck in there!" he panted, steering his fellow refugee toward a black alley mouth. "Quick!"

Don, obedient to the command and the pressure on his shoulder, swerved sharply in his dash and plunged into the alley, Abel close after him. There the two came to an abrupt halt, peering up the dim street they had just quitted for sound or sight of Desmond.

But no tread reached their ears in the evening stillness nor did the few lights from houses reveal any skulking shadows drawing in on them. Simon Peter, who had been galloping ahead of his masters, noted the cessation of their steps and came trotting inquiringly back. Abel caught his collar and pulled him into the alley.

"There!" whispered Herrick. "We've thrown 'em off the track for a while, anyhow. From here we c'n see anybody comin' upstreet or downstreet from either way. This alley's blacker'n the street. If anyone passes along, all we've got to do is to sneak down the alley. It's too dark in here for us to be seen. If—"

"Then we'll wait here awhile and if we find no one's after us we'll go back and look for Colonel Branch's house and—"

"Donny!" groaned Abel, his disgust almost making him forget to whisper. "Donny! That's what you git by fillin' your head with movies instead of hoss sense. D'you want us to run spang into them fellers' hands? Huh? Do you?"

"But—" began the bewildered Don.

"Don't you see how it all come about?" insisted Abel. "Desmond got ashore somehow or other. Most likely he was able to swim to a gob of wreckage after the dinghy upset. Then some of them search parties found him and set him ashore at Gattysville here. Or else they set him ashore somewheres upstream and he come here because he had pals here. He was a-settin' in the hotel to-night, all sore over losin' that precious bag of his'n. Then in comes we, and he hears us ask how to git to Colonel Branch's house. Yes, and he hears the man tell us how to—if Desmond didn't know already where 'twas. The second we go out he lights out after us, maybe sendin' some pal to watch the other end of the square or to stand in front of the colonel's house in case Desmond misses us in the dark. Then he overhauls us and gits the bag. Then Simon Peter here overhauls him and gits back the bag for us and we skip. Well, what then?"

"Well," echoed Don crossly, "what then?"

"We give him the slip," explained Abel, in growing impatience at the other's denseness. "What does he do? He knows where we was bound for. He knows we was aimin' for Colonel Branch's house. Any feller he may have sent ahead to keep watch there would tell him we hadn't got there yet. So what would he do? He'd just lay in waitin', close to the house, till we show up, and then nab us. And yet you want to bungle up there and git cotched like a blind hen in a coop! Gee, but—"

"You're—you're right!" exclaimed Don, ashamed of his own stupidity. "Dead right, Abe. That's exactly where he'll be waiting for us. And he heard us speak about going back to the hotel afterward. So he'll have an eye on that too. We'll have to stay where we are till daylight and then—"

"And then walk right into him when we go anywhere near Colonel Branch's house or the hotel or the bank!" finished Abel. "No, no, Donny! This town's a heap too small to hold us, safe, just now. We don't know who's in cahoots with him and who ain't. These crooks travel in gangs, I've heard tell. That Lee Hotel may be one of their hang-outs. They may start a-combin' the whole town for us. They know their way round here, most likely. And we don't. They'd have us by the heels in no time. We—"

"What—what are we going to do, then?" asked Don, trying to steady the nervousness out of his voice. "If we can't go to the colonel's or to the bank or to the hotel—and if it gets to be daylight, so we can't be hidden any longer—"

"We've got just one thing we can do," announced Abel. "I've got it all figgered out. We'll get back to the raft—if we can do it without anyone seein' us—and we'll cast off and set that motor of your'n to workin' overtime. And we'll pike downstream lickety-split till we git to Annsburg. We'll hang onto the bag, too, till we git there, then turn it over to your dad. It's the only safe chance we got. What d'you say?"

"I say, yes!" decided Don with no hesitation. "Oh, Abe, if it wasn't for you I'd be making a fool of myself every seven minutes till I got—"

"If 'twasn't for you," countered Abel, generous in his expansion under Don's praise, "if it wasn't for you we'd 'a' lost that table long ago. We'd have had no fire if you hadn't thought of the burnin' glass. Desmond would 'a' killed Simon Peter and nabbed the two of us when he come aboard that night if you hadn't knocked his knife away. And—I'd most likely have hung onto this money for myself if you hadn't 'a' showed me it wa'n't our'n. I guess the two of us is a pretty fair team, Donny. What one's got the other ain't. And 'tother way round. Let's let it go at that and quit jabberin' like Sunday-school books. We—"

"All right," agreed Don, glad to shift from anything bordering on sentiment. "Suppose we make tracks for the raft."

"S'pose we don't," said Abel. "We're safe here. Anyhow, we c'n see anyone comin' along the street before they c'n see us. Here's a good place to lay low till Desmond and them has a chance to hunt themselves tired and to figger we're camped down somewheres for the night or else that we've left town. In a small place like this we'd be likely to run into 'em if we start out while they're still searchin'. Let's stay here till long about 'leven o'clock—till folks is abed. Then we c'n git to the raft a lot safer."

So for two or three interminable hours the boys crouched dolefully in the alley mouth, Simon Peter snoozing beside them on the damp ground. One or two people strayed past during their wait. But these evidently were looking for nothing and were homegoing townsfolk. Except for shrinking farther back into the alley's gloom and holding shut the collie's jaws to keep him from growling, the boys did not let these passers-by ruffle their calm.

At last they stole out into the silent street, and moving stealthily along riverward, halting at every faintest sound, they crept down the thoroughfare to the water's edge.

The raft was not there!

In the momentary pause of consternation they heard a light and hurrying footfall on the street behind them.

"We're goners, I reckon!" whispered Abel in his friend's ear. "Raft gone, Desmond behind, river ahead. We're cornered all right!"

## Chapter X

FOR answer Don dropped noiselessly behind a pile of salvaged barrels that blocked most of the street end. He drew Simon Peter into the impromptu hiding place along with him. Abel broke off in his own muttered lamentation at their plight and scuttled, ratlike, behind the nearest barrel.

The hurrying step came closer. The boys held their breath and lay flat in the mud behind their barrels. Abel, peeping out through a chink between two of the casks, could see the dim figure of a man outlined against the murky sky.

The man seemed gigantic. In his hand he swung something that looked like a bludgeon.

He halted, for an instant, not three feet away from Abel's barrel. Then, turning on his heel, he sauntered back the way he had come. Between his teeth he was even humming a scrap of a tune.

The country boy, unversed in the ways of towns, had no way of recognizing the stick-swinging stranger as one of the special watchmen detailed to patrol the water front at night, when floods have cast ashore valuable flotsam that requires time for moving and which offers temptation to river thieves. This particular watchman was evidently in a hurry to finish his rounds, for he had cast but the most fleeting glance at the array of barrels.

For five minutes after his departure neither of the boys spoke. Then came Don Page's whisper through the darkness.

"Abe!" he called softly. "These barrels must have been here all day. They're dry. If they'd been hauled out of the water to-night—since we got to town—they'd still be soaking wet. So—"

"S-s-h!" warned Abel nervously. "This yer's no time for jabberin'. We—"

"But don't you see?" persisted Don, crawling nearer. "If these barrels have been here all day, this can't be the street where we landed. And," with sudden inspiration, "of course it isn't. We landed at the foot of the street that had the station and the hotel on it. And the man at the hotel sent us to Beauregard Street—the next street back of that one. That's the street we're at the foot of now—Beauregard Street. If we hadn't been scared stiff we'd have remembered that. So before we give up the table for lost let's look for it at the place we left it—not a square to the north."

"Shucks!" snorted Abel, forgetting caution in a gust of self-contempt. "Who's the fool now? It's me! Good for you, Donny! Come along!"

Still carefully and in silence, but with higher hearts, they emerged from their concealment, waking the bored Simon Peter from a comfortable doze with what seemed to him an unnecessary suddenness.

Two hundred feet downstream they came upon the raft, safe moored where they had left it. Pausing only to listen for any recurrence of those mysterious footfalls, the trio scrambled aboard and thrust the table free from the bank.

Not until poles and oars had carried them well out into the current and a mile below Gattysville did they venture on the use of the noisy motor. For more than an hour thereafter they stared tensely upstream in their own wake or listened, above the engine's purr, for sounds of any pursuing boat.

But a little after twelve they divided the rest of the night into three-hour watches. Abel took the first. At three he awakened his dead-tired chum, who, after his one experience in sleeping at his post, knew he could rely on self-respect to keep him awake for the coming vigil.

When Abel awoke at sunrise Don was still alert, if haggard, at the steering wheel.

Stoutly he refused to turn in for an hour's doze and he insisted on helping Abel prepare breakfast. Five minutes later Abel found him asleep on the deck, one cheek pillowed bumpily on a pile of potatoes he had begun to peel.

Abel grinned down at the slumberer, then took off his own jacket and laid it gently over the snoring boy's shoulders, as protection from the raw river wind of early morning.

Some time afterward a squawking flock of tame ducks, washed down river by the flood, swam athwart the raft's round prow, splashing wildly in their haste to dodge the awkwardly moving table. Simon Peter took their antics as a challenge to his own dignity and rushed to the raft edge, whence he launched at the skittering flock a volley of thunderous barks.

Vibrant with indignation, the collie hurled all the power of his lungs into the salvo of defiance. Before Abel could quiet him, the din awoke Don, who sat up rubbing his eyes and looking foolish.

"I—I must have dropped off asleep for a second," he apologized. "I—"

"Went to sleep, hey?" laughed Abel. "Must 'a' been just a cat nap then. You was peelin' potatoes last time I looked at you. Finish your snooze. Breakfast won't be ready for fifteen minutes, yet."

Don sank back, grateful for the chance of another doze. But as he relaxed he chanced to notice the coat flung across his shoulders. He eyed this wonderingly for an instant. Then he looked at his watch. With a jump he was on his feet.

"I've slept a solid hour!" he cried. "You old liar, you tried to keep me from feeling bad about letting you get breakfast all alone! And you've been shivering because you put your coat over me! I've a good mind to lick you for that!"

"You never saw the day you could lick a quarter section of me!" retorted Abel. "You derned city cuss, you couldn't fight hard enough to keep yourself warm! Now gimme back that coat of mine you stole when I wa'n't lookin'. Then wash up for breakfast. Gee, but you got a dirty face on you! How far d'ye reckon we are from Annsburg?" he continued, having sheered the talk from sloppiness. "The river's fell quite a piece in the night. Lots of landmarks and things on shore now that ought to tell you something of where we are. Take a squint round."

It was half an hour after midday when an impossible craft chugged wallowingly in an oblique angle from upstream and bore down upon a docklike structure which jutted from the water at the foot of Annsburg's chief business street.

This building, in normal times, was the town's largest storage warehouse. It stood on piles at the water front; at present its flat roof and about ten inches of upper wall were all that showed above the surface of the river.

To the roof wharf the table raft wallowed its erratic way. As Don brought the raft neatly alongside, Abel Herrick cast her painter loop over a staunch low chimney which rose above the shoreward corner of the submerged roof.

"Allow all the rope you can!" directed Don from the wheel. "This roof's fully twenty feet high. When the river goes down we don't want to have the table hanging in mid-air from the chimney. Put a second rope round that iron bolt yonder and allow a good twenty feet leeway on both of them. Then she'll stay here for further orders, I should think."

By the time the raft was tight moored there were a score of Annsburg people on the flat roof and more were running down the street toward the new arrivals. Someone, from higher in the town, had sighted the circular motor craft as she warped into her queer dock. He had called the attention of others to the uncanny sight. And a handful of idlers had come down to the water to investigate.

A bank clerk on his way back from lunch paused to look at the two young mariners. Then without a word he turned and raced like mad up the street toward the bank.

President Page had that morning returned home for a few hours, in an interval of frantic search of river and banks for his missing son. He was even now waiting impatiently at the bank for a reply to his telegrams requisitioning additional tugs. Already six tugs and thirty men were scouring the Mississippi, from Wyckoff, south, for sign of Donald.

The only passenger on any of these tugs was a square-faced man whose iron jaw was less steady than usual as he scanned the wreckage-strewn waste of waters for his boy.

Abel Herrick's father had hurried to Annsburg the moment he heard of the tidal wave that had swept the fair into the river. Train service was suspended and the farmer had come to town to hire a tug in which to hunt the Mississippi and its banks for his son. He found Page had already chartered every boat of the sort. But on telling his story to the banker, Herrick had received ready permission to go as a passenger on the fastest of the tugs.

Into the bank president's private room burst the breathless clerk. Before he had panted out two sentences of his message Mr. Page had darted from the room and was rushing down the street at a most undignified pace for so portly a citizen, scattering people from his path and dodging under the noses of automobiles in his headlong flight. Out of breath and with his heart hammering against his ribs, he gained the warehouse roof and broke through the crowd that surrounded the two boys. Don caught a fleeting glimpse of his father as the banker bore down upon him with outspread arms.

"We've brought your directors'-room table home safe to you, sir!" sang out the boy, inordinately proud of the achievement. "And this is Abe Herrick, my bunkie. He's a brick! He—"

But a mighty bear hug from his half-crying, half-laughing father shut off the rest of the boy's jubilant speech.

The two boys several hours later were seated in state in the president's private office at the Annsburg bank. Between them on the floor sat Simon Peter, very much at home and very friendly with everybody. Simon Peter had received much praise and much petting and much food since his arrival in town that day and he was reveling in the ovation that was his.

Seated also in the private office were Mr. Page and three other Annsburg dignitaries, one of them the local chief of police. On the table in front of them lay the black bag, wide open, its contents strewn round it.

The chief of police was in the midst of a discourse which he addressed to the two boys rather than to the president. The news brought was the result of an automobile trip he and two deputies had taken the moment Don and Abel had disclosed the tale of the bag. The motor trip had been to Gattysville, fifteen miles to northward. The chief had just returned.

"Yes," he was saying, "he's the man, all right. I knew he must be when you youngsters told me about him. The same man. Here's the idea— Ritter has done one term in Federal prison, already, for the same kind of thing. He—"

"Who's Ritter?" interrupted Abel. "We didn't meet any Ritter. We—"

"Ritter is the man you boys knew as Claude C. Desmond," explained Page.

"This is fair month, all through the South and Southwest," explained the chief. "A bumper time for counterfeiters. Ritter and some pals of his are counterfeiters. No-good ones, at that. They faked some thousands of dollars in counterfeit bills and Ritter went out with the stuff to get rid of it. Some secret service men got after him at the Wyckoff Fair. The flood saved him from them. He escaped to high ground when the wave hit the fair. Then he started south. They were after him.

"At last he tried to shake them off by commandeering a small boat and trying to cross the Mississippi in the dark one foggy night. They were close behind him and they overhauled him in a motor boat. They fired over his head two or three times to make him halt. Then they bore down on his boat. It was empty. He had gone overside in the fog. They cruised round looking for him. But the fog was too thick. He boarded your raft. In the night he escaped in a dinghy. The dinghy upset against a log or a reef and he had to swim for it. A search party picked him up and set him ashore on the west bank. From there he worked his way to Gattysville. At a hotel there he saw you lads, and he saw you had the bag. He tried to get it from you but your dog was too much for him. So he—"

"But how do you know all this?" queried Donald in amaze.

"Oh," laughed the chief, "I had a little confab with him. And he came through—told me, I mean. It seems he broke his wrist and got concussion of the brain when your dog landed on his back."

"Hold on!" begged Abel confusedly. "Wait a second! Let me git this straight. Is all this—this fortune—is it—is it all counterfeit money?"

"Every cent of it is counterfeit," said the chief. "Mr. Page told you that already, didn't he? It—"

"And folks who try to pass counterfeit money gets sent to jail?" pursued Abel.

"They sure do!" affirmed the chief. "Good and plenty. Why?"

"Then," said Abel, shivering a little in retrospective terror, as he glanced guiltily at the wriggling Don, "then, if we'd done like we wanted to and kept this cash—then we'd 'a' gone to prison, first time we spent a dollar of it! Say, Donny! It—it pays to be—to be square, after all."

Mr. Page and the chief exchanged glances. The chief cleared his throat, then said:

"That's right, sonny. The money was N. G. as long as you hung onto it. But it isn't quite N. G. now. That bag of queer bills was the evidence the Federal people needed to convict Ritter. You lads have supplied the evidence. The government had offered a $500 reward for evidence to convict him. It looks to me as if that $500 would have to be split up between you two."

The two boys looked at each other a long minute, dazed. Then Don beckoned Abel out of the office and onto the front steps of the bank. At a snap of his finger, Simon Peter followed.

"Say!" he began, his hand on the collie's head. "Father's promised me he'll find Simon Peter's owner and buy Simon Peter from him, no matter what it costs. Now here's a bargain I'll make with you. If you'll give up your share of Simon Peter to me and let me keep him here at Annsburg, I'll give up my share of the $500 reward to you. Is it a deal?"

"No!" refused Abel vehemently. "It ain't. Simon Peter is as much mine as he's yours and he's done just as much for me as he's done for you. You c'n keep all the reward. I want to keep Simon Peter. Besides, the city's no place for a big dog.

"It's just like when your dad tole me awhile back, to-day, that he'd give me a fine chance in the bank and send me to business college if I'd stay here with you-all. You heard me tell him that my dad says there's more of a future for a man in the right kind of farmin' than in any city, didn't you? Well, it's the same with Simon Peter."

"I've as good a right to him," began Don hotly, "as you have and I'm—"

He broke off with a gurgle. The dog had wandered idly from the steps to the side-walk and from the curb out into the street. A motor car, whizzing round the corner, bore down on him. Instinctively, the dog leaped aside, barely in time to avoid the flying wheels.

The leap carried him directly in front of a heavy motor truck. He shrank back in confusion and fear, just as the truck's wheel grazed his furry side. Then he fled toward the boys for protection.

As he galloped toward them, mouth open, eyes frightened, an hysterical woman caught sight of him as he flashed past her. She screamed:

"Mad dog!"

A passing policeman whipped out his revolver and leveled it at the luckless collie. But the pistol was not fired. For two ragingly indignant boys flung themselves between their pet and the arm of the law. Then they led Simon Peter back to the bank. At the threshold, Don paused.

"You're right, Abe! The city's no place for a big dog. Not if we love the dog. Take him to the farm with you when you go. He's yours. But you'll take your half of the reward too."

"He'll keep on b'longin' to both of us," decreed Abel, as the other's voice thickened. "Only he'll live out to the farm. You are comin' out every week to see him. Likewise, I'm comin' to Annsburg as often as I c'n do it, to see you. This trip has taught us a lot, I'll say," continued Abel, his mind on the fortuneless fortune.

"That's so," assented Don, with memories of his own vanished snobbishness. "And it's been worth it. I wouldn't have missed it for a thousand dollars. And"—he added reflectively, "I wouldn't go through it again for a million—with Simon Peter thrown in for good measure!"


## The End

# Afterword

## by Kathryn D. George

"The Flood Fighters," which appeared in serial form in *The Country Gentleman Magazine* from July 10 through September 11, 1920, is unique among the hundreds upon hundreds of magazine stories written by Albert Payson Terhune, as it is the only known instance of his magazine fiction written under a pseudonym. Terhune himself never admitted to being the author of the story. We know for certain that he was because of an extant letter written by his wife, Anice Terhune, two years after Bert's death, wherein she disclosed the true identity of "Stephen Dirck."

Why might Terhune have chosen to remain anonymous with this particular story? We can only speculate on possible reasons. The simplest explanation might be that it was a test: Would readers relish a collie story by the unknown "Stephen Dirck" the way they did ones written under Terhune's own name? Was his name the draw on any given story with his byline? But remember that this was still fairly early in his dog writing career. From the first appearance of the "Lad" stories in January of 1916 until June of 1920, his dog stories in magazines numbered fewer than two dozen. His first two dog books, *Lad: A Dog*, the runaway bestseller published in April 1919, and *Bruce*, published in March of 1920, were, for the most part, merely compilations of those magazine short stories.

The mass appeal of his collie fiction, and the fame and endless requests for more and more dog stories that came with it, were in the earliest stages, so there had to be more to the reason behind his need to be "Stephen Dirck." Adding to the mystery is the fact that four installments of another serial, "Buff: A Collie" ran under Terhune's own byline in the same issues of *Country Gentleman* as four of the installments of "The Flood Fighters." Was this a red herring, to make readers think that Terhune and Dirck were two separate writers, or, with the ability to see the two side by side for stylistic comparison, was it a clue to Dirck's true identity? The observant reader might also note that the two stories shared the same illustrator, Frank Stick, and the illustrations in both stories depict collies with identical markings.

The inclusion of "Buff: A Collie" brings up another possible explanation for the use of a pseudonym, that being the reluctance of magazine editors to run two stories by the same author in the same issue. However, this too can be discounted. First, Terhune had already made a name for himself in the world of pulp fiction writers. His name was well-known to readers of the day; as such, it is highly unlikely that Terhune would have allowed a magazine to run a story written by him under another name. He would have wanted to see his name *twice,* or would have requested that the story simply appear in another issue. *The Country Gentleman* was owned by the Curtis Publishing Company, which also owned *The Ladies Home Journal* and *The Saturday Evening Post.* A quick search through Terhune's body of magazine work shows nine separate instances of two stories running under his byline in one magazine, and all were for the Curtis Publishing Company. Clearly they had no problem with Terhune's name appearing twice in one issue. Might there have been a reason?

A look at the *Country Gentleman* masthead for the issues in question shows the Managing Editor and Art Editor were Barton W. Currie and Loring A. Schuler, respectively. Currie and Schuler were longtime friends of Terhune, as all three worked together at the *New York Evening World.* Terhune most likely had met Currie as far back as 1905, when both worked under the infamous Charles Chapin. In *To the Best of My Memory,* Terhune included both Currie and Schuler in a group of men he considered journalistic greats that he worked with at the *Evening World* from 1911 to 1916, saying that he considered them to be "the premier staff in newspaper history." The depth of their friendship is shown in Terhune's dedication of *The Man in the Dark,* which came out in book form in February 1921, to Currie. A decade later, he would dedicate *A Dog Named Chips* to Schuler. It does appear that Terhune wanted the story to run under a pseudonym. Knowing their personal and professional relationship, it then becomes easy to imagine Terhune asking them for a "small favor," and making the request to run "The Flood Fighters" under a pseudonym to appear simultaneously with "Buff: A Collie." So that leaves us to find another answer.

One possible, and in this case, most probable, answer is that what he was writing was too controversial to run under his own name. But "The Flood Fighters," on its surface at least, is simply a story about two boys and a collie helping each other through a bout with the wrath of Mother Nature. Nothing controversial in that…or is there? In *To the Best of My Memory,* Terhune told of the ghost-writing efforts of his early career, and how he would sprinkle the work with clues to prove that he had been the actual writer. It might be the name of one of his dogs, or someone he knew in his small hometown of Pompton Lakes, New Jersey. In "The Flood Fighters" he also sprinkled clues throughout the story, instantly recognizable to anyone who had read his collie fiction or knew some of his personal information.

Clues to the writer's true identity are sprinkled throughout the story. The first clue is to be found in the name of Abel Herrick. Herrick was Terhune's sister Christine's married name. Transpose the first letters of Albert and you get Abel. His wife Anice, whom he affectionately called Annie, was born and raised in Hampden County, Massachusetts. Annsburg and Hampden County feature prominently in the story.

Three of the Sunnybank collies, Lad, Gray Dawn, and Wolf, are obliquely referenced: "the bemused *lads,*" "At *gray dawn,*" and in, "Heroism consists in hanging on one minute longer," a favorite Terhune line that would have been instantly recognizable to anyone who had read "One Minute Longer" in the December 1919 *St. Nicholas Magazine.* The hero of that story was Wolf, who saved a boy from drowning, very much a parallel to what was happening in "The Flood Fighters."

Anyone familiar with the Terhunes, their dogs, and his stories probably would have recognized some, if not all, of the clues. So what message might Terhune have been sending, why, and to whom, in writing as "Stephen Dirck"?

The summer of 1919 had found Terhune in the middle of a maelstrom of bickering within the collie fancy. His own breeding program was in its infancy; up to that point, there had only been two Sunnybank litters. He was known within the fancy more for his collie stories and the subsequent sales they brought to the established breeders than for his kennels. In a private letter, which Terhune subsequently gave permission to publish in *Field and Fancy,* he took the collie fancy to task for their infighting and lack of unity, deploring their behavior as unsportsmanlike and curiously unique to the breed. In the fall of 1919, one of the most prominent collie breeders of the day, Dr. O.P. Bennett, disagreed with him in print. Having just returned from the war in Europe, Bennett hoped to find "peace and harmony" at home, but instead found "unsettled conditions," and what he called a "terrible indictment" of the collie fancy by Terhune. Even though Bennett wrote a few months later that he would "feel badly indeed to have anything I have said or done cause him to lose interest in them or the fancy," Terhune's resulting disillusionment with the pettiness and backbiting of the breeders of the day nearly led him to leave the Collie Club of America.

"The Flood Fighters" may have been a more subtle attempt at getting his message across to them, or was perhaps an exercise in catharsis for him. There is much that is symbolic in this story, too. The first clue to Dirck's identity is the careful choice of the pseudonym. Terhune was a man of deep faith, fiercely proud of his Dutch heritage, with a passion for collecting antique armaments. In the Bible, Saint Stephen was judged for his words, and subsequently stoned to death. Dirck is twofold in meaning—spelled Dirck, it is a Dutch name. Its homonym, dirk, is a Scottish thrusting dagger. Here was a symbolic name that said it all: a Dutchman, judged and attacked for his words, thrusting back with a dagger.

The title itself is also telling—Terhune was fighting a flood of criticism at the time. His story carries a definite message. It is about the silliness of petty arguments, about the importance of working together and learning from each other, as we each have something to impart. Symbolism abounds throughout. The redwood can be viewed as a symbol of strength and healing, of wisdom and longevity; an ark in the chaotic flood, the ark itself a symbol of new beginnings.

Another interesting symbol is the snake, which can symbolize vengefulness, the enemy, the devil, or it can be the complete opposite, a symbol of healing. But the fact that the snake depicted in the story is one looking to devour the boys and the dog lends weight to its being a symbol of vindictiveness. It is the collie who kills the threatening snake by breaking its back, risking his own existence for the two boys he worships, but who just can't seem to agree on things.

Veiled meanings can be gleaned from the main characters' names as well. Donald is derived from "world ruler," and was the name of two kings of Scotland, where the collie breed originated. Abel, in addition to being an anagram of sorts for Albert, has the biblical story behind it of the younger brother slain by the older brother—which could signify a parallel to Terhune, new to the collie fancy, being attacked by its elder statesmen. Yet the shortened "Abe" carries with it its own connection to a man Terhune greatly admired: Abraham Lincoln, who brought an end to the Civil War. The Civil War is also slyly referenced in the "Lee Hotel" in "Gattysville."

The most symbolic name, however, is that of Simon Peter, the collie lost in the flood. Here once again, Terhune makes an important biblical connection. Simon Peter is another name for Saint Peter, to whom Christ said, *Thou art Peter, and upon this rock I will build my church,"* another fairly blunt message to the fancy that the collie should be their focus; that they should work together to build up, not tear down, their magnificent breed. The message is reinforced when Don and Abel elect Simon Peter to be "captain of our galleon."

But there is more to the backstory of this, as an event occurred that might very well have helped to inspire Terhune's tale, and which might give weight to the theory that the story was a message of sorts to the collie fancy. At 3 a.m. on the morning of February 4, 1920, rain began to fall in New York City. By 3:30 it had turned to sleet, and by 7:30, the city was being blanketed by snow. Over a period of 76 hours, a mixture of rain, sleet, and snow fell, leaving the city streets encased in a veritable parfait of seventeen and a half inches of frozen multi-layered ice and snow. It was so severe that the U.S. Army was called in to try and melt the snow and ice from the streets using flamethrowers. *The New York Times* called the aftermath of the storm a "plow-proof, pick-proof, shovel-proof, flame-proof stratum of ice." The Collie Club of New York's Specialty Show was scheduled for February 10th; the 44th Annual Westminster Kennel Club Show was scheduled to begin the day after—and New York City was icebound.

One of Bennett's allies in the ongoing argument with Terhune was prominent breeder Edwin L. Pickhardt. Traveling from Wisconsin to New York through the storm, Pickhardt's collies were lost in transit, much like Simon Peter is separated from his owner during the storm and resulting flood. Hearing of Pickhardt's dilemma, the collie fancy responded with a seemingly newfound spirit of unity and cooperation. Judging was delayed or rescheduled to allow Pickhardt's entries to make their way to the show. When Pickhardt's dogs finally arrived, the collie folks pitched in to get them as ready for the ring as they could. It was a testament to the collie fancy that all had put aside any differences and worked together under these most difficult circumstances, not only for the Specialty Show but also for Westminster.

Based on what Terhune observed at the two shows, perhaps there was a reason for his writing the story other than a poke at the collie fancy or personal catharsis. Could it have been a peace offering, the symbolic dove returning to the Ark with an olive branch to signal that the flood was finally subsiding? What comes to mind are Lincoln's words after the end of the war: "With malice toward none, with charity for all…"

Whether or not the collie fancy took note of his story and its message is unknown, but what is known is that by August of 1920, all was apparently forgiven. Terhune not only remained a member of, but became more involved with, the Collie Club of America. O.P. Bennett wrote in *Dogdom:*

> I do feel that the collie fancy owe a debt of gratitude to Mr. Terhune for the interest he is creating in this breed. Every day or so I receive a letter from a prospective customer telling me they have just read "Lad: A Dog" or "Bruce," and are desirous of purchasing a collie. Such stories as Mr. Terhune writes bring the collie before the public and create more interest in them than thousands of dollars spent in advertising would do.

In the ensuing years, Terhune, Bennett, and Pickhardt would form a mutual admiration society of sorts, not only working together as colleagues, but becoming good friends. Bennett thought highly enough of the quality of Terhune's Sunnybank Kennels that, when the second edition of his classic book, *The Collie,* was published, he included some of the Sunnybank dogs. Pickhardt, in writing his own book, *The Collie in America,* asked Terhune to write its Introduction.

Albert Payson Terhune never used the name "Stephen Dirck" for a work of fiction again. He did, however, resurrect him for a highly personal essay about facing death titled, "I Set My House in Order," published in 1936. Here was another instance of Terhune needing to say something, yet wishing to remain anonymous. And, true to form, clues to his real identity were sprinkled throughout the article. There is, however, one interesting passage that belies his "Flood Fighters" message of setting aside petty differences:

> There are a few—a very, *very* few—people with whom I am still on passing bad terms. Perhaps the fault is mine. Perhaps it is theirs. What does it matter whose fault it is? In each instance it is a perfectly good grudge. As such it stands; and thus it shall stand (as far as I am concerned) until doomsday.

But, he also wrote that he did not "pretend to be a patient and smiling saint." He was the first to admit that he was human. And, since he says that there were only "very, very few" with whom he still held a grudge, we can assume that he did his best to follow his own advice, and set aside petty differences whenever possible. We are fortunate that the events of 1919 did not turn him from the collie fancy, as Terhune went on to become a respected breeder and judge in his own right, deepened his friendship with both Bennett and Pickhardt, and of course, continued to write the stories that enamored us all of the collie.

We cannot be absolutely certain of Terhune's reasons for writing as "Stephen Dirck" for "The Flood Fighters"—again, we can only speculate. But as Abe says at the end of "Flood Fighters," "This trip has taught us a lot."

Kathryn D. George
August 2015

www.ingramcontent.com/pod-product-compliance
Lightning Source LLC
Chambersburg PA
CBHW071010120726
47910CB00004B/1463